Just like having a heart-to-heart with
your best friend, these stories will take you
from laughter to tears and back again!

Curl up and have a

Heart *to* Heart

with Harlequin Romance®

So heartwarming and emotional
you'll want to have some tissues handy!

Look out for more stories

in **HEART TO HEART**

coming soon to

Harlequin Romance®

Dear Reader,

I do like a good dose of royalty. Not day-to-day, opening fetes and greeting-dignitaries-type royalty, but castles and footmen and glass coaches—the full fantastic fairy tale. Wouldn't it be fun to be a part of it for a while?

Oh, I hear you say, but it surely never happens in real life. Normal people don't find themselves in the middle of such a soap bubble. But what if...what if...?

That's where I come in. I can't resist a good romance and here we have two lovely people— normalish people even if Raoul's a wee bit gorgeous—catapulted into wonder.

It's fun, it's fantastic and I believed every word of it as I wrote. I did enjoy donning a tiara, and I trust you'll enjoy wearing one, too.

Marion Lennox

Sit back and enjoy this wonderfully emotional new story from award-winning author Marion Lennox.

PRINCESS OF CONVENIENCE

Marion Lennox

Heart *to* **Heart**

HARLEQUIN®

TORONTO • NEW YORK • LONDON
AMSTERDAM • PARIS • SYDNEY • HAMBURG
STOCKHOLM • ATHENS • TOKYO • MILAN • MADRID
PRAGUE • WARSAW • BUDAPEST • AUCKLAND

ISBN 0-373-18230-9

PRINCESS OF CONVENIENCE

First North American Publication 2006.

Copyright © 2005 by Marion Lennox.

www.eHarlequin.com

Printed in U.S.A.

Marion Lennox was born on an Australian dairy farm. She moved on—mostly because the cows weren't interested in her stories! Marion writes for the Medical Romance™ and Harlequin Romance® lines. In her non-writing life Marion cares (haphazardly) for her husband, kids, dogs, cats, chickens and anyone else who lines up at her dinner table. She fights her rampant garden (she's losing) and her house dust (she's lost!). She also travels, which she finds seriously addictive. As a teenager Marion was told she'd never get anywhere reading romance. Now romance is the basis of her stories; her stories allow her to travel, and if ever there was one advertisement for following your dream, she'd be it!

In *Princess of Convenience* Marion takes us into a wonderful mix of reality and fairy tale; where Jessica finds there's more to this royal business than meets the eye, and her royal prince finds his thoroughly modern princess is more likely to wear Wellingtons than glass slippers.

You can contact Marion at www.marionlennox.com

CHAPTER ONE

SHE should be driving on this side of the road. Surely?

This was the most fabulous autoroute in Alp'Azuri. The road spiralled around snow-capped mountains, with the sea crashing hundreds of feet below. Every twist in the road seemed to reveal postcard magic. Medieval castles, ancient fishing villages, lush pastures dotted with long-haired goats and alpacas—every sight was seemingly designed to take the breath away.

The twist she'd just taken had given her a fleeting glimpse of the home of the Alp'Azuri royal family. Made of glistening white stone, with turrets, towers and battlements and set high on the crags overlooking the sea, the castle looked as if it had been taken straight out of a fairy tale.

Two years ago Jessica Devlin would have been entranced. But now she was concentrating on reaching the next of her suppliers—concentrating on not thinking about the empty passenger seat—concentrating simply on staying on the right side of the road.

She was sure she was on the right side of the road.

The autoroute consisted of blind bends winding

around the mountain. As she drove, Jess caught sight of the road looping above and below.

The road above was the worry. Was she imagining it?

She drove cautiously around the next bend and caught a glimpse of a blue, open-topped sports car. The car was two curves above. Coming fast.

Driving against the cliff edge.

Her side.

Surely it should be on the other side?

She braked hard, turning her car onto a slight verge between cliff and road. The bend ahead was blind. If the car ahead came round on the wrong side...

It had to be her imagination. She was basing this fear on a flash of blue, now out of sight.

Maybe the driver ahead had better vision of the road than she did. She was being too cautious.

But she still felt the first claws of fear. Too much had happened in her life to trust that the worst wouldn't happen now. Thus Jess was almost stopped when the blue car swept around the bend. Travelling far, far too fast.

On her side of the road.

She was as far onto the verge as she could be without melting into the cliff. There was nowhere she could go.

'No.' She put her hands out, blindly. 'No.'

No one heard.

Today was meant to have been his wedding day. Instead...it made a great day for a funeral.

'Do you suppose she meant to do it?' Lionel, Archduke of Alp'Azuri, looked at the flag-draped coffin with distaste. He was supposed to be supporting his great-nephew in his grief, but neither man could summon much energy for strong emotion.

There'd been too much grief in the past few weeks for another death to destroy them.

'What, kill herself?' Raoul, Lionel's great-nephew, didn't even try to sound devastated. He sounded furious, which was exactly how he felt. 'Sarah? You have to be kidding.'

This was crazy, he decided. What on earth was he doing here, playing the wounded lover at the funeral of his fiancée?

But he knew his duty. Raoul, Prince Regent of Alp'Azuri for at least another six days, stood at rigid attention while his fiancée was committed for burial, but all he felt was distaste.

'She had what she wanted,' he told his uncle, and there was no way he could disguise his anger. 'She was drunk, Lionel, and it was only because the woman she hit was an incredibly careful driver that she didn't manage to take someone else with her.'

'But why?' Lionel was clearly at a loss.

'She had her girlfriends here for a pre-bridal lunch. Then she decided to drive down to Vesey to meet her lover. Her lover! Six days before the wedding, with every camera in the country trained on her. Do you know what her blood alcohol content was?'

'Raoul, look distraught,' his uncle hissed. 'The cameras are on you.'

'I'm suffering in stoic agony,' Raoul said grimly. 'All the papers say so. Just as well she crashed before she met her latest interest.'

'Hell, Raoul…'

'You want me to be sympathetic?' Raoul demanded. 'Oh, you know I didn't want her dead but I never wanted to marry her. She might have been a distant cousin but I hardly knew her. This was your idea. Of all the stupid…'

'I thought she'd be OK,' Lionel said, and if the cameras were on his face now they would certainly see distress. 'Sarah was brought up to royalty. She knew what was expected of her. She could handle the media.'

'So well that she managed to disguise the fact that she had a lover she intended keeping. How long would the marriage have lasted before the media found out?'

Lionel hesitated. 'I suspect that Sarah didn't think you'd care.'

'You know I wouldn't. But the media is a different matter.'

'They understood. It was a marriage of convenience. Such things have been happening in royal families forever, and every person in this country wants you to marry.' Lionel grimaced. 'Except your cousin, Marcel. Why you've held out for so long before marrying… Hell, Raoul, it puts us in an appalling position.'

'Not me,' Raoul said grimly. 'I've done enough. I'm out of here.'

'Which leaves your nephew—and your country—

where?' Lionel cast a nervous glance at Sarah's family, who seemed to be arguing over whose flower arrangement would take precedence. 'In the hands of yet another like your brother—another government puppet. The only thing that could have saved us was this marriage.' His grimace grew more pronounced. 'Look at that. Her family are like vultures.'

'They are vultures. They wanted this marriage because of the money.' Raoul glanced at his once prospective in-laws with the air of a man who'd seen his destiny and escaped by a hair's breadth. 'That was all Sarah wanted. Money and power and prestige. She would have screwed this principality.'

'But not as much as our prime minister and Marcel.' Lionel sounded morose. 'So it was a mistake. But now…'

Raoul stared grimly at the coffin. 'I've done as much as I can. You'll have to take over. Exert some influence over Marcel.'

His uncle forgot about looking bereft and just looked appalled. 'Me? You have to be joking. I'm seventy-seven, Raoul, and Marcel hasn't listened to me for forty years. You know he and his wife don't want the boy. Sure, anyone who takes on the prince regent role has to be married, but married or not, Marcel and Marguerite are no more fit to be parents than…well, than your brother and his wife. Begging your pardon, Raoul.'

'You don't have to beg my pardon. Jean-Paul was a dissolute fool, just like my father.'

'Your father was my nephew.'

'Then you knew how inexcusable his conduct was,' Raoul said savagely. 'And what he left of the royal family were exactly the same. Jean-Paul, Cherie and Sarah. My brother, his wife and my cousin. Now they're all dead, two from taking pure heroin instead of the normal dope they've been living on for years, and one from drunken speeding on her way to meet a lover. And now Sarah's death means that Marcel takes control. God help this country and God help the crown prince. But there's nothing more I can do now, Lionel. I want out.'

'Your mother—'

'My mother is the reason I agreed to marry Sarah. She wants the child.' He hesitated. 'But there's nothing more I can do. She can't have him.'

'No,' Lionel said reflectively and turned to where the dignitaries were attempting to reason with Sarah's family. 'It looks like Marcel will take him, and you know Marcel is a government puppet. They'll never let your mother have access.'

'I can't help that,' Raoul said roughly. 'I've done my best.'

'Choosing Sarah wasn't your best.'

'Lionel…'

'OK, I helped choose. I concede she wasn't a great choice but you hardly gave us time. Now we've got six days.'

'To find a bride so I can stay on as Prince Regent? You have to be kidding.'

'If she'd just waited to kill herself until the week

after the wedding rather than the week before...' Lionel sighed. 'But she didn't. We're in a mess, boy.'

'We are at that.' Raoul grimaced and then put a hand on his uncle's shoulder, as if gaining support and strength from his elder. He almost visibly braced himself.

'Enough. I'm going to put my flowers on Sarah's coffin.'

'Because you want to?'

'Because her mother and her father and her ex-husband and two of her lovers are all out there threatening to kill each other if I don't,' he said grimly. 'It's time for a man to take a stand. I'll put flowers on Sarah's grave, I'll do the best I can to see my mother has access to her grandson and then I'm going back to my medicine in Africa. Where I belong. This royalty business is for someone else. I resign.'

For the first two days after the accident Jessica was asked no questions. Concussion, shock and the anaesthetic she was given for a dislocated shoulder were enough to send her drifting into a space no one could reach.

After that she was aware of questions being softly asked. Not too many, but essentials for all that. The questions were asked first in English, and then as those around her realised she spoke their language, in the soft and lilting mix of French and Italian used throughout Alp'Azuri.

Who was she?

That was easy. 'Jessica Devlin.'

Where was she from? Her passport said Australia. Was that right?

'Yes. I'm Australian.'

Who did she want them to contact?

'No one. Unless I'm dead, in which case my cousin, Cordelia, but don't you dare let her know where I am if there's the slightest chance that I might live. Please.'

After that they backed off a bit—these gentle people who nursed her. Who were they? She didn't ask.

There was a woman with elegant clothes and silver hair and a worried look that seemed to be more worried every time she saw her. There was a silver-haired old gentleman who deferred to the lady. He called her ma'am and carried in trays and he also looked worried.

Who else? Two nurses—one at night, one during the day, and a doctor who patted her hand and said, 'You'll be fine, my dear. You're young and you're strong.'

Of course. She was young and strong.

The doctor asked the hardest question and that was the only one that she had real trouble making herself answer. When the nurses and the others were gone the doctor touched her gently on the hand and asked, 'Girl, your child. Your family. I have to know. There was no sign of anyone else in the car. There's no wedding ring on your finger, but there are signs on your body that tell me you've had a child. There wasn't a little one in the car, was there?' His face stilled as he prepared for the worst. 'No one else went over the cliff?'

She fought to answer that. Fought to say the words. But they had to be said to stop this kindly old doctor panicking more. He had no need to fear the worst. The worst had already happened.

'I only have… I've only *had* the one child and he's dead. Back in Australia. Before I came here.'

There was a pause. Then, 'Maybe you're not so young after all,' he murmured. 'My dear.'

But her eyes had closed and he let her be. He didn't intrude. None of them did. They let her lie in this luxurious bed draped in crimson velvet and gold tassels, sinking into a mattress that felt like clouds, and they let her sleep.

She'd hardly slept since Dom died, she thought drearily in one of her tiny lucid moments. It was as if her body was now screaming at her that it had to catch up.

She slept and slept and slept.

On day six—or was it day seven?—she opened her eyes and for the first time she really looked around her. Until now she'd simply accepted this bed, this room, the astounding view through her casement windows as the next in a series of events fate was throwing at her. She'd been out of control for so long that she'd ceased asking questions.

Now, though, sunlight was streaming in over sumptuous furnishings and she gave herself up to astonishment. This was no hospital.

The nurses were no longer here. Now there was only this fairy-tale bedroom and an elderly lady, sitting by the window gazing out at the morning.

Was she crying?

'What's wrong?' Jess asked and the lady turned, sadness replaced by concern in an instant.

'Oh, my dear. It's not you who should be asking that.'

Jess gazed cautiously around her. She'd been awake but not awake. In some dream world. Taking the time out she so desperately needed. 'I guess I should have been asking questions before now,' she tried. 'Like… where am I?'

'This is the royal palace of Alp'Azuri.'

'Right.' Jess let that sink in for a while. Alp'Azuri. She knew she was in Alp'Azuri. This tiny country was famous all over the world for its fabulous weavers and she'd come here because…

Because of fabric and yarns. She thought about it, remembering a long-ago conversation with her cousin, Cordelia. 'You take the trip, dear. Research your suppliers on the ground. It'll take your mind off things best forgotten.'

Things best forgotten. Dominic?

This wasn't the time to be thinking of Dom.

'Um…why am I in the royal palace instead of a hospital?' she asked, and grief washed back over the older woman's face.

'Do you remember the accident?'

'I…' Jess swallowed. She did remember. The sports car coming fast. Unbelievably fast. It was right in front of her and all she could do was put up her hand and say…

'No.'

Then as the lady winced, thinking she'd have to start at the beginning, she corrected herself.

'I do remember a little. I remember a blue sports car on the wrong side of the road. At least I think it was on the wrong side.'

'That was Sarah's car,' the lady said. 'Lady Sarah Veerharch was my son's fiancée.'

Jess swallowed. There was something about the lady's face that made her not want to go on, but she had to. Even though she already knew the answer. *Was*. The woman had said *was*. 'I... Sarah was...killed?' How had she made herself say it? And to her horror the woman was nodding.

'She was killed instantly. Her car glanced off yours—the fact that you were able to stop before the cars hit apparently saved your life—but Sarah slewed off the cliff and into the sea.'

'No.'

'I'm sorry, my dear, but yes.'

Jess's eyes closed in anguish. So much death. It followed her everywhere. Dominic, and now this...

Concentrate on practicalities, she told herself fiercely. If you think about death you'll go quietly crazy.

'So why am I in a royal palace?' she asked and the lady's face grew grave.

'This is my home. Mine, my son's and my grandson's. For...for now. There's such media coverage—such interest. Dr Briet thought that, seeing your injuries were relatively minor, you'd be better off here where we could protect you from the worst of it.'

'Such media coverage.' Jess's face had lost whatever colour it had. 'Lady Sarah... Your future daughter-in-law. Your son's the...'

'Raoul is the Prince Regent of Alp'Azuri,' his mother told her. 'At least... Well, for now he is. I'm Louise d'Apergenet. My son is Raoul Louis d'Apergenet, second in line to the crown. He is... He *was* to succeed to his position as regent on the occasion of his marriage. Which was to have been yesterday.'

'And I've killed his bride.' Jess's voice subsided to an appalled whisper.

'Sarah killed herself. You had nothing to do with it.'

The strong male voice startled them both. Jess's gaze flew to the open door.

She hadn't seen this man before. Nurses, doctor, servants...this man fitted none of these categories.

He was...royal?

Royalty was her first impression and maybe it wouldn't have been her first impression if she wasn't sitting under a velvet draped canopy in a fairy-tale castle. He was wearing light chinos, a dark polo shirt and faded loafers. These were casual clothes, but there was nothing casual about this man.

Tall, dark, superbly muscled, the man's strongly-boned face was lean, appearing almost sculpted. His eyes were hawk-like and shadowed, revealing nothing. But indefinable or not, the aura of power he exuded was unmistakable.

Was he really a prince? His skin was weathered to

a deep bronze, his eyes were creased as if accustomed to a too-harsh sun and there was a long, hairline scar running the length of his jaw. And his hands... These were no prince's hands. They'd worked hard.

There was no trace of easy living on this man's frame. Jess stared up at him, stunned. Even a little afraid?

But then he smiled—and the fear evaporated, just like that.

You couldn't fear a man with a smile like this.

'Good morning,' he said softly. 'You must be Jessica. How are you feeling?'

'I... Yes. I'm Jessica and I'm fine.' Unconsciously her hands tugged her bedcovers to her chin, in a naïve gesture of defence. Why? He didn't make her feel afraid, she thought. He just made her feel—small? Young? In her flimsy cotton nightgown, with her short crop of chestnut curls tousled from sleep and her freckled face devoid of make-up, she felt about twelve.

'I'm Raoul,' he told her.

She'd guessed. 'Y... Your Highness.'

'Raoul.' His voice firmed, and there was even a tinge of anger, as if he was repudiating something he found offensive.

'Jessica's been fretting about Sarah's death,' his mother told him. 'I've told her she's not to blame herself.'

'How can you blame yourself?' Raoul was speaking in English. His voice was strong and deep, and only faintly tinged with the accent of his native country.

Where did he fit in? How did this family fit into the government of this place? Jess thought, trying desperately to remember what she'd learned of this country before she came here. Not much. Her trip this time been more an excuse to get away than to learn about another culture, and her only other visit here had been fleeting and had ended in disaster.

But she knew a little. Alp'Azuri was a principality, a tiny country edged by the sea. There'd been some recent tragedy, she thought, remembering flashes of international news in the past few weeks. A dissolute prince and his princess found dead. A tiny crown prince, orphaned.

Where did that leave Raoul?

'I'll not have you blaming yourself for Sarah's death,' Raoul was saying, and she blinked, trying to haul herself back to reality. To now.

'Um…'

'Sarah killed herself.' Raoul's voice was stern, sure of what had to be said. 'Oh, not intentionally. We're sure of that. But she'd been drinking. She was driving too fast on the wrong side of the road and the police say the only reason you weren't killed also was because you were being incredibly cautious. Somehow, miraculously, you managed to avoid a double tragedy.'

'But if I hadn't been there…'

'Then she might have hit someone else further down. Maybe with even worse consequences.' He shook his head. 'If it had been a family…' He closed his eyes, as if to shut out a tragedy that could have been. 'We're all grateful that you were there, Jessica, and that you somehow prevented what could have been a lot, lot worse.'

'But your fiancée...'

'Yes.' His eyes were open again now, and behind their cool, appraising look she could see pain. And something else. Despair? Defeat? 'But we move on.'

'Edouard will stay with me,' his mother said softly and Jess frowned at this strange twist in the conversation. 'We will fight for him. We must.'

Jess was lost. Edouard? Fighting?

Was this yet another tragedy? She pulled her covers even higher, in a gesture of protection that was as crazy as it was unhelpful.

'I've been lying here for too long,' she managed and Louise smiled.

'My dear, it's been six days. You were concussed and you dislocated your shoulder. But Dr Briet says—and Raoul concurs—that you seem to have been suffering more than that. He says you seem exhausted. You were taken initially to the Vesey hospital but when it was clear that all you needed to do was to sleep, it seemed best to bring you here.' She hesitated. 'It's not possible to keep the Press away anywhere else, and Raoul has been on hand if needed.'

This was making less and less sense. 'You've been very good,' Jess managed, 'in the face of your own tragedy.' She hesitated, but there was more to be said. Edouard. The name had brought back a memory now, remembrance of news reports she'd read surely less than a month ago. 'And it's not just Sarah, is it?'

'You can't know…' Louise started but Jess was too distressed to stop.

'I'm remembering the deaths of the crown prince and his princess,' Jess said. 'And your grandson being orphaned. I heard of it back in Australia. I'd just… forgotten.'

Of course. When her own world had collapsed, so had her ability to take in tragedies of those about her. But the deaths had been front-page news at home at a time when her world had been blank and meaningless, and it had been dreadful enough to haul her out of her pool of misery, into someone else's.

She remembered cringing inside. The prince and his princess, in a chalet high in the mountains. An avalanche? A storm? She couldn't remember. But she remembered that the child was alive, unharmed, but with his parents both dead.

The world had been captivated.

Deep in her own personal tragedy, Jess had hardly taken it in. But now… She forced herself to think back to those half-remembered newspaper headlines. Rumours that it hadn't been a storm that had killed them. That the storm had cut off access to the cabin and meant that normal checks couldn't be made. The royal couple had escaped their minders and there'd been drugs.

This was not her scene, she told herself fiercely. It was not her business.

She looked up at Raoul and there was that look on his face that precluded questions—and how to ask a question like the ones that were forming in the back of her mind? She couldn't. She didn't need to. Thankfully.

She was so tired.

She lay back on her pillows and closed her eyes, allowing the exhaustion and distress to wash through.

Unexpectedly Raoul stepped forward and lifted her hand. The gesture was a measure of comfort that was surprisingly successful. It was strong and reassuring and compelling. 'Don't distress yourself,' he told her. 'You mustn't.'

His touch warmed her more than she'd thought such a gesture could. It was unexpected, a gesture that he didn't need to make. Maybe in the same circumstances she'd find it impossible to make this gesture herself, she thought. To touch the cause of more sadness…

'Jess, you're not to focus on this,' he told her, his voice, like his touch, strong and warm and sure. 'You're here as our guest for as long as you need before you feel strong enough to face the world.'

'I'm well now.' She opened her eyes and he was close, she thought, dazed. Too close.

'You've had a hell of a time,' he told her. 'And maybe not just this week?'

It was a question. She swallowed. This man was wounded too, she thought.

'We're a pair,' she whispered and there was a stillness.

'I…'

'I'll leave you as soon as I can pack,' she said wearily. 'I'm fine. It was very good of you to let me stay this long.'

'Jess, as soon as you leave this place you'll be in-undated,' he said warningly. 'The world's Press want interviews. This tragedy has caught the attention of the international media and you won't be left alone. Plus after six days in bed you'll be as weak as a kitten. Stay here. Within the walls of this castle I can protect you. At least for the next few days. Outside...I'm afraid you're alone.'

Silence.

Within the walls of this castle he'd protect her?

It was crazy. She didn't need protection.

She couldn't stay.

Where could she go?

Home?

Home was where the heart was.

She had no home.

'Stay for a few more days.' It was Louise, gently adding her urging to her son's. 'We feel so responsi-ble. You have no idea what the Press will be like. You seem exhausted. Let us give you just a little time out.'

Time out.

It was an idea that was almost incredibly appealing. And it was the only thing she could think of to do. What else? Pick up the threads?

What threads?

She was bone-weary and she was faced with a choice. These pillows and the protection of castle walls for a few more days—or the scrutiny of the world's Press. There was suddenly no choice. Especially as Raoul was smiling down at her like... like...

She didn't know. All she knew was that his smile warmed parts of her that desperately needed to be warmed. Stay? Of course she'd stay.

She must.

'Thank you,' she whispered, and she was rewarded by a widening of that killer smile.

'Good.' Raoul's voice was strong again, commanding and sure. His eyes met hers, filled with warmth and pleasure that she'd decided to be sensible. 'Join the world slowly again, no? Start with dinner tonight. With us.'

'I...'

'It's very informal,' Louise told her, guessing immediately the confusion such an invitation would cause. 'Just my son and myself.' She smiled, and her smile was ineffably sad. 'And the odd servant or six.'

'Have just Henri serve us tonight, Mama,' Raoul told her. 'Give the other servants the night off.'

She nodded. 'That would be lovely. If you don't think it's cowardly.'

'Maybe we need to be cowardly,' he told her. 'Maybe we all do. For a while.'

CHAPTER TWO

JESS wallowed—that had to be the word for what one did in such a sumptuous bathtub—and thought about what she was about to experience.

Dinner with the Prince Regent of Alp'Azuri...

As a little girl she'd read the tale of Cinderella—of course she had—and she'd dreamed of princes. But now...

Reality was very different, she thought. Real princes weren't riding white chargers ready to whisk a woman away from the troubles of the world. Real princes came with tragedies of their own.

It made the whole situation seem surreal, so much so that as she dried and dressed, slowly, in deference to her aching muscles and myriad scratches, she didn't cringe that she had no fabulous evening gown to wear, or a fairy godmother on hand to transform her.

She should wear severe black, she thought, but she shoved that thought aside as well. Black? When had she ever?

At least she had her stock-in-trade—the reason she was in this country. Her wardrobe had been brought more to show suppliers what she wanted than to wear herself. Tonight she chose a simple skirt, cut on the bias so it swirled softly to her knees. The skirt combined three tones of aquamarine, blended in soft waves. The colours were almost identical but not quite, and when spun together they were somehow magical. She teamed the skirt with an embroidered, white-on-white blouse with a mandarin collar and tiny sleeves. It hid her bruises perfectly.

That was that. No make-up. Like black, make-up was also something she didn't do. Not since long before Dominic.

She brushed her close-cropped chestnut curls until they shone, then gazed at her reflection in the mirror.

These were great clothes, she conceded, but it was a pity about the model. This model had far too many freckles. This model had eyes that were too big and permanently shadowed with grief.

The model needed a good...life?

'You've had your life,' she told her reflection. 'Move on. They're waiting for you to go to dinner.'

But still she gazed in the mirror, and something akin to panic was threatening to overwhelm her.

This was a suite of rooms. 'It's one of several guest suites we have, dear,' Louise had told her. It consisted of a vast bedroom, a fantastic bathroom and a furnished sitting room where the fire had crackled in the hearth the whole time she'd been here, its heat augmenting the spring sunshine that glimmered through the south-facing windows. The windows looked down over lawns that stretched away to parks and woodland beyond.

The whole place was breathtakingly beautiful, yet

until now Jess had simply accepted it as it was. It was as if her mind had shut down. For the last few days she'd simply submitted to these people's care.

Now she had to move. She'd said she'd go to dinner. She was dressed and ready. But outside was a castle. A castle!

How had Cinderella coped with collywobbles?

But then there was a knock on the door and Henri was there. The elderly butler was someone she was starting to recognise, and his smiling presence was steadying and welcome.

Her own private fairy godfather?

'I thought I'd accompany you down, miss,' he told her, his twinkling eyes letting her know that he recognised her butterflies and that was exactly why he was here. 'It's easy to get lost in these corridors.' He surveyed her clothes with approval. 'And if I may say so, miss, you look too lovely to lose.'

Jess smiled back, knowing if she was inappropriately dressed he would have warned her, but his smile said she was fine. He held out his arm and she hesitated a little and then stepped forward to take it. Yep, he was definitely a fairy godfather and she wasn't letting go of his arm for anything.

'You know, they're just people,' he told her as they started the long trek toward the distant royal dining room. 'They're people in trouble. Just like you.'

That initial time Jess had seen Raoul—the one time he'd entered her bedroom—she'd thought he was stunningly good-looking. Now, as Henri opened the dining-room door, she saw he was dressed for the evening, and good-looking didn't come close.

The cut of his jet-black suit and his blue-black silk tie clearly delineated his clothes as Italian-designed and expensive. The crisp white linen of his shirt set off his deeply tanned skin to perfection. And his smile…

Good-looking? No. He was just plain drop-dead gorgeous, she decided. Toe-curlingly gorgeous.

Henri paused at the dining-room door, smiling, waiting for Raoul to react. And he did. He rose swiftly, crossed to take her arm from Henri's, led her to her seat and handed her into it with care.

It's just like I'm a princess, Jess thought, and she even managed to get a bit breathless. OK, she'd been shocked into a stupor where she'd hardly noticed her surroundings these last few weeks, but there were certain things that could pierce the thickest stupor.

Raoul Louis d'Apergenet was certainly one of them.

Her outfit was too simple for this setting, she thought fleetingly, with a tiny niggle of dismay, but Raoul was smiling at her as if she was indeed a princess and Louise was gazing at her skirt with admiration and saying,

'Snap.'

'Snap?' Jess sat down—absurdly aware of Raoul's hands adjusting her chair—and gazed at the array of silver and crystal before her. Snap? Card games was the last thing she was thinking about.

The table must be one of the palace's smallest. It

was only meant for eight or ten—but it was magnificent. The array of crystal and silverware made her blink in astonishment.

'I think the word is wow,' she said softly. 'Snap has nothing to do with it.'

'I meant your skirt.' Louise was still smiling. 'If I'm not mistaken that's a Waves original. The same as mine.'

Jess focused—which was really hard when there was so much to take in. And when Raoul was smiling with that gentle, half-sad smile, the smile that said he knew…

She was being ridiculous.

Louise's skirt. Concentrate.

Her hostess was indeed wearing a Waves skirt. It was one of Jess's early designs, much more flamboyant than the one she was wearing, a calf-length circle of soft spun silk, aqua and white, the colours mingling in the shimmering waves that were Jess's trademark— the colours of the sea.

'I love the Waves work,' Louise was saying. 'And you must, too. But then you're Australian. Waves is by an Australian designer, isn't it?'

'Yes,' Jess said and then because she couldn't think of anything else to say she added, 'Um, she's me. Waves, that is. It's what I do.'

'You work for Waves?'

'I am Waves,' she said a trifle self-consciously. Actually, until a year ago she wouldn't have said that. She would have said she was half of Waves. But then, that had never been true. She'd supported Warren, and when she'd needed him…

No. She closed her eyes and when she opened them Henri was setting a plate before her.

'Lobster broth, miss,' he said and it gave her a chance to catch her breath, to look gratefully up at him, to smile and to recover.

'I own Waves,' she told them, conscious of Louise's eyes worrying about her and Raoul's eyes… doing what? He seemed distant, assessing, but then maybe he had room for caution. 'I started designing at school and it's grown.'

'You're not serious? You own Waves?' Louise's expression was one of pure admiration. 'Raoul, do you hear that? Waves is known throughout the world. We have a famous person in our midst.'

'I'm hardly famous,' she managed. She tried the broth. 'This is lovely,' she told Henri, though in truth she tasted nothing.

'Are you here on a holiday?' Raoul was gently probing, his eyes resting on her face. He seemed to be appraising, she thought, as if maybe he suspected his mother needed protecting from impostors and she might just be one.

She was being fanciful.

'I… No. I'm here on a fabric-buying mission.'

'There was no fabric in your car,' Raoul said.

Once again, that impression of distrust.

'Maybe because my plane landed the morning of the crash,' she told him and there was an edge to her voice that she hadn't intended. She tried to soften it.

'I'm here to buy but I've hardly started. I'd heard that the Alp'Azuri weavers are wonderful and the yarns here are fabulous.' She hesitated but couldn't help herself. 'I have already been to one supplier. If you've searched my luggage you'll have found yarns.'

'I didn't search your luggage,' Raoul said, swiftly, and Jess raised her brows and managed a slight, disbelieving smile. Good. It was good to have him defensive.

Why? She didn't know. And maybe she was being dumb. To get a European prince of the blood offside...

Whoa, Jess. Back off.

'My son didn't mean to be offensive,' Louise was saying and to Jess's delight Raoul was getting a look of reproof from his mother. Hey, she'd won this round. 'And the Alp'Azuri spinners certainly are amazing.' Louise was animated now as if here at last was a safe subject, a subject they could indulge in where everything wasn't raw. 'I could take you out and introduce—'

'No, Mama,' Raoul told her. 'You can't go out. Not while there's this drama. You forget.'

His mother flushed and bit her lip. 'No. I'm sorry.'

'Are the Press hounding you?' Jess looked from one to the other, her spurt of childish satisfaction fading. Their faces were tight with strain. She'd been so caught up in her own misery that she'd hardly noticed, but she was noticing now. There was more behind these expressions than their recent tragedy, awful as that was.

'The Press are certainly hounding us,' Raoul said heavily. 'They're waiting for us to leave.'

'We need to leave the castle eventually,' Louise whispered. 'We can't stay here indefinitely.'

'Why would you want to leave?' Jess said, astonished.

'We're a bit under siege,' Louise said and then bit her lip and looked ruefully at her son. 'I'm sorry,' she said again. 'I didn't... Jess, you're not interested in our troubles.'

'Too many troubles,' Raoul muttered. 'None of our making. Drink your soup, Jess. Forget it.'

But it seemed that trouble couldn't be forgotten. Henri re-entered the room almost as he said the words, and he wasn't bearing food. He looked distressed.

Definitely trouble.

'I'm sorry, sir,' he told Raoul, 'but your cousin, the Comte Marcel, is here. He's been here three times today already and this time he refuses to leave.'

'Of course I refuse to leave.'

The voice was a ponderous, pompous baritone, and before Henri had time to withdraw, the dining-room door was shoved wide. Henri was shoved roughly aside. 'This is my home from now on, man,' the newcomer said. 'You and my so dear relatives will just have to grow accustomed to it. Now.'

Was it possible to take a dislike to someone on sight? Whether it was the imperiousness of his tone, the audacity of his statement or the way he'd shoved Henri, Jess's first reaction was revulsion. She wasn't alone in her reaction. Raoul was rising to his feet and his face was dark with anger.

'What the hell do you think you're doing, shoving your way into my mother's dining room?' he snapped and the man's eyes rose in supercilious reproof.

'Surely you mean *my* dining room.'

He was in his late fifties, short and balding, with what was left of his hair oiled flatly down over a shiny scalp. He was dressed in expensive evening wear but his clothes weren't flattering. His stomach protruded over his sash, and nothing could disguise the flab beneath the suit.

'This is my husband's nephew, the Comte Marcel d'Apergenet,' Louise murmured to Jess, and there was real distress in her tone now as she attempted introductions. 'Raoul, please sit down. Jess, this is the…the new regent as of next week. Marcel, this is Jessica Devlin.'

The man's eyes were already sweeping the room. They flickered over Raoul with dislike, they moved past Louise with disdain and now they rested on Jess with something akin to approval.

'Ha. The girl who killed Lady Sarah.'

'She did not kill—' Louise started hotly, but the man held up his hands as if to ward off attack. He even smiled.

'Now, even if she did, who am I to criticise? Sarah might have been a distant relative but she wasn't close. Are any of our family close? No. And her death destroyed your plans very neatly. But that means we need to move on. I've been trying for days to see the pair of you, but your damned butler refuses me admission. It's time to face the future.'

'No.' Louise's voice broke on a faint sob. 'Sarah's only been dead for six days. And Edouard's so traumatised. Marcel, surely you mean to give us time.'

'Monday's changeover,' the man snapped. 'No matter who's dead. You know the terms of the regency. I take over the castle and I take over responsibility for the child until he's of an age to accept the crown. You left this country twenty-five years ago and you have no place here. Our politicians agree with me. They want you out of here, and the regency is mine.'

There was a deathly silence, and then Louise seemed to brace herself. 'My grandson stays with me,' she said but her voice faltered as if she knew already what the response would be.

'Like hell he does.' The man smiled again, and Jessica shivered. She didn't have a clue what was going on but the more she saw of this man the more she wanted to cringe. 'The constitution says that the role of regent can only be held by a married man,' he said. His tone had slowed now, as if he was speaking to a group of imbeciles. 'The incumbent to the regency has to take over within a month of the death of the monarch, and if he can't do it by then, then the next in line to the throne—the next married man—takes over. I therefore have complete constitutional control, including custody of the crown prince and residency of the castle. I want you out.'

'Not until Monday.' Raoul looked as if he wanted to hit someone. Badly. His hands were clenched into fists and his voice was laced with the strain of keeping himself under rigid control. 'You get nothing until Monday. Not until the month is legally up. Meanwhile this place is our home and you have no place in it.'

'The child would be better handed over immediately,' the man snapped. 'I have staff waiting to care for him.'

'He'll stay with me,' Louise said with distress, but Marcel smiled still more.

'Not unless there's a constitutional change and there's no way a constitutional change can take place without the approval of the prince regent. Which would be me. You know the rules. You tried to avoid them by a hasty marriage, but Lady Sarah's death has ended that. The child will be raised as I decree.' Once again his hands were raised, as if to ward off objections that might occur to them. His smile became almost a smirk. 'You need have no fear. Every care will be taken of him.'

'You mean you'll let the government do as they want with him just as long as they keep your coffers filled.' Raoul's voice was barely a whisper, but there was no disguising the fury behind it. 'You'll destroy him, just as you and my father destroyed my brother.'

'He's such a little boy,' Louise stammered. 'He's three. Marcel, you can't take him away from his family.'

'I'll take him anywhere I want. I have that right.'

'Not until Monday, you can't.' Raoul's rigid control had snapped. 'You bottom-feeding low-life, you have no right to be here and I'll not accept your presence here a moment longer.'

'You can't—'

'Watch me.' With no more hesitation, Raoul walked steadily forward and gripped his relative's collar in both his hands, lifting him right off the floor. He swung him around and shoved—hard.

'Get your hands off me.' Marcel's voice was an indignant splutter.

'This is our home. Until Monday you don't have any say in who enters here.'

'That's in less than a week. This is preposterous.' But he was out the door and still being propelled. 'I'll have you arrested.'

'Try it.'

Jess could no longer see what was happening. Raoul had kept propelling, out into the hall and further toward the grand entrance.

She didn't understand.

She turned to Louise—but Louise was crumpling back into her chair. Her hands were up to her face and she was weeping.

'Louise.' Dignity or not, royalty or not, Jess was crouching beside her, hugging. Louise responded with a shattered sob as she subsided into Jessica's shoulder. She only sobbed out loud the once but Jess could feel as the shuddering sobs continued to rack her frail body.

Louise was far too thin, she thought. She was gaunt, as if this suffering was nothing new. She'd lost a son and a daughter-in-law less than a month ago. Then she'd lost Sarah. And now...

Somewhere there was a little boy who was being threatened.

She'd never seen a child here.

Still, until tonight she'd never been out of her suite of rooms.

'Will you tell me what's happening?' she asked, but Louise couldn't answer.

Henri was fluttering uselessly behind them and Jess could see that he was just as distressed as Louise. 'What's wrong?' she whispered, and a tear rolled unchecked down the elderly man's wrinkled cheek.

'It's the little prince,' Henri murmured, looking down in concern at Louise. 'Ma'am...'

'Mama.' Raoul was back with them, kneeling beside Jess and his mother. He took his mother's shoulders in his big hands, transferring her weight to him.

There was such gentleness here, Jess thought as she moved aside. He was a big man; he'd handled Marcel with barely suppressed violence, yet he held his mother with absolute love.

'Mama, we'll think of something,' he was saying, whispering softly into her hair. 'We'll take it to the courts. They can't enforce this.'

'They will,' his mother said brokenly. 'You know there's no access at all to the crown prince by anyone other than his legal guardian. When your father and I split up I wasn't allowed near Jean-Paul. God knows I tried.'

'This is crazy,' Jess said, not wanting to interrupt

such distress but overcome by her urge to know. 'Can someone tell me what's happening?'

'It's easy, miss.' It was Henri, speaking up behind her as Raoul hugged his mother. The elderly servant had stared down at the pair of them and then he'd turned away. Maybe talking to Jess helped. Or maybe it was that he couldn't think of what else to do. 'Or…maybe it's hard.'

'I don't understand.'

'Do you know that if a ruling monarch dies and the heir is still a child, then the appointed prince regent is responsible for raising him? And making decisions in his stead?'

'That's right,' Jess said, thinking it through. 'I've read that. It's to stop a child king—or a crown prince in a principality—having responsibility too young.'

'That's right.' Henri gave a wintry smile. 'But the rules in this country are hard. Prince Raoul is second in line to the throne after Edouard, so Prince Raoul would normally be prince regent, but, as he's not married, he's not eligible. The rules are rigid. Cruelly rigid.' He hesitated and glanced again at Louise and Raoul—but Raoul was deeply enmeshed in his mother's distress and had no room to listen to what his butler was saying.

'In truth, the Prince Raoul hardly wants the role,' the butler told her. 'Since the Princess Louise separated from the old prince, she and Prince Raoul have not been permitted to come here. They've made their home in Paris, and lately Prince Raoul has been working overseas. But for the child's sake, and for the country's sake, Raoul decided to return. Lady Sarah agreed to marry him so he could take on guardianship of the child, the idea being that Her Highness would take care of her grandchild. But then Lady Sarah was killed.'

He hesitated again but then he shrugged, as if he'd decided that having gone this far, he might as well go all the way. 'You must realise that Lady Sarah was no better than she ought to be,' he said softly. 'She was the prince's cousin, and she agreed to the marriage merely for the money and prestige it would bring. Unfortunately she didn't have the sense to stay alive to enjoy the consequences.'

There were places she didn't want to go, Jess decided as she thought this through, and Sarah's death was one of them. There was too much to think of here already. But the child… The little prince…

'I haven't seen a child here,' Jess whispered. 'Where is he?'

'Edouard's a quiet one,' Henri told her. 'He's little more than three years old and he's not very strong. He'll be well asleep by now. And he doesn't know his grandmother enough yet for her to spend much time with him. He's very, very nervy.'

'But the Princess Louise wants to keep him?' She shook her head, bewildered. 'Why doesn't she know him very well? I don't understand.'

'I'm not surprised,' Henri said grimly, with a sideways glance at the two bowed heads. Raoul was still intent on his mother's grief and was taking no notice—and Louise seemed to be taking nothing in. 'But maybe it's not so uncommon. Marriages splitting; children being raised apart. Raoul was just six years old when his parents' marriage failed. The old prince was only interested in his heir, so Princess Louise was permitted to take her younger children away with her. But Raoul's older brother was kept here, and Her Highness was granted no access. It's been breaking her heart for over thirty years over the son she left behind, and, for the last three years, for the grandson she wasn't allowed to know. And now the tragedy continues. Prince Jean-Paul grew up wild and unfettered and he died because of it. Now it seems that that Princess Louise's grandson will grow up in the same sterile environment. The Comte Marcel is just as…devoid of morality as his cousin; his wife's no better, and they care for nothing but themselves. The whole country knows it. Everyone here wanted Raoul to return. But now he can't. And our little prince is lost.'

There was surging anger in the elderly man's voice and he'd forgotten to speak in an undervoice. Unnoticed, the sobs had stopped. Louise had heard.

'So now you know,' she told Jess, her voice breaking in despair. 'Sarah's death is only a tiny fragment of our tragedy.'

'I'm so sorry,' Jess whispered and Louise's face crumpled again.

'I wish I'd never married into this family,' she whispered. 'Despite my children. My wonderful children and now my grandson.' She broke away from

Raoul and rose on feet that were decidedly unsteady. 'I've let them all down and I can't bear it.'

'Mama...' Raoul started but she shook her head.

'Enough. I need my bed. Jess, I'm so sorry your first dinner up was so badly interrupted. But you'll have to excuse me.'

'I'll take you,' Raoul told her but once again she shook her head.

'No. You stay and take care of Jess. Henri, can you escort me upstairs? I think...I may need your arm.'

'Certainly, Ma'am,' Henri said.

This was a long-standing friendship, Jess realised. It was not just a mistress-servant relationship. Henri moved forward and took the support of Louise from Raoul. The two silver heads moved together in mutual distress and together they left the room.

Jess was left staring after them.

With Raoul.

There was a long silence. An awful silence. Jess could think of nothing to say.

Finally she caught herself. She had no place here in these people's troubles. They were in distress. She needed to leave.

'I'm so sorry,' she murmured. 'I'll leave first thing in the morning. I'm only adding to your troubles by staying.'

'You're not adding to our troubles.' She saw Raoul almost visibly stiffen, moving on. 'It's me who's sorry,' he told her. 'We invite you to dinner, and here our soup's cold and Henri's gone. I'll try and find someone to bring something more.'

She looked at him, appraising. He'd missed out on his dinner, too, she thought. Food. When she was in deep trouble she remembered kindly people forcing her to eat and she knew that sometimes it helped.

'Could we give the servants a miss?' she told him. 'You show me a kitchen and I'll feed myself.'

'What?' He almost sounded astonished.

'You do have kitchens in palaces?' she said in an attempt to keep it light. 'You have toasters and bread and butter? And marmalade? I'm particularly partial to marmalade.'

He stared some more—and then the corners of his mouth twisted in a crooked smile as he realised what she was doing. She was doing her best to convert tragedy to the domestic.

'I'd imagine so,' he managed. 'I've never investigated.'

'You live here and you've never investigated the kitchen? You don't even know if there's marmalade?'

'I've only been here for two weeks,' he said, his smile fading. 'I came to prepare for the wedding. After that I was going straight back to...to work.'

'With your bride?'

'Sarah was a bride of convenience,' he said stiffly, his smile disappearing altogether. 'It was a business proposition. I had no intention of staying here.'

A business proposition. She stared at his face and there was nothing there to show what he was thinking. Just the cold words: a business proposition. And then he was leaving. Leaving his mother with the child? Leaving his bride?

Running?

'Were you afraid to stay?'

Why had she said that? It had just slipped out and it was unfair. She knew it as soon as she had said it and she bit her lip in distress. 'I'm sorry. It's just…'

'If you meant was I leaving the care of my nephew to my mother, maybe I was,' he told her. 'But my mother wants to be here. I don't.'

She was puzzled. 'Even if you'd become regent? Wouldn't that be a cool thing to be? A real royal?'

'I intended to take care of the business side of the job from a distance. I'm certainly not interested in the ceremonial duties.' He shrugged. 'So no, it wouldn't be cool. Not that it matters. I'm no longer in line for the job.'

Trouble slammed back with a capital T—and Jess took a deep breath and decided the only option here was to return to what she knew.

Food. Marmalade.

She actually was hungry, and she bet this man was, too.

'So let's find the kitchen,' she suggested. 'Do you really not know if there's marmalade?'

'No, I…'

'You've been in a castle for two weeks and not explored?'

'Why would I want to explore?'

'Why would you not?' she asked in astonishment. 'A real live palace. A royal residence. I'll bet you run to six types of marmalade, Your Highness.' She smiled at him, teasing, trying to elicit his smile again.

There was so much going on in this man's life that light-hearted banter seemed the only way to go. 'You know, I'll bet you have a whole team of cooks lined up in the galley, ready with the next eleven courses of our twelve-course feast.'

'I'm sorry to disappoint you,' he told her, 'but, if you recall, we've given the servants the night off. My mother was desperate for a little quiet, and thus we had only Henri. And I'm not Your Highness. I'm Raoul.'

'So Henri's been cooking—Raoul.'

It was odd calling him Raoul. There was a barrier between them that she seemed to be stepping over every time she smiled. And she stepped over it a lot more when she called him by his name.

Maybe he was aware of it, too. His tone had become strangely stiff and formal. 'I gather the cook pre-prepared things but essentially yes,' he told her, 'Henri was cooking. Maybe I can contact the cook and ask her to come back.'

'Why?' Jess frowned—and then sniffed. And thought about the sequence of events until now. 'So Henri was cooking. And now he's taken your mother up to her apartments,' she said. Still sniffing. 'Your Highness—sorry—Raoul, I hate to say it but we may have a mess in the kitchen.'

'How on earth…?'

'How on earth do I know that?' She even managed a grin. 'Pure intelligence,' she told him and sniffed again. 'Sherlock Holmes, that's me. The Hound of the Baskervilles has nothing on my nose. And you know something else? I figure that even if you don't know where the kitchens are…'

'I do know that.'

'Even if you don't, then I can follow my nose,' she told him. 'There's something burning and I'm betting it's our dinner. Let's go save your castle from conflagration. That seems a really essential thing to do and, in times of trouble, essentials are…essential.'

CHAPTER THREE

THEY walked down a long corridor and through four arches. 'You know, it's amazing the soup was still warm by the time it reached the table,' Jess said. 'No wonder Henri's thin. The poor man must walk a marathon every day.'

Raoul didn't smile. He was preoccupied, Jess knew, and all she could do was try and keep it light.

When they finally reached the kitchen there wasn't a conflagration, but there was Jess's predicted mess. Henri had obviously just put the steak on when their unwelcome visitor had arrived. There were three plates laid out with a salad on the side, but now the steak was sending up clouds of black smoke and a saucepan of tiny potatoes had boiled dry. The potatoes were turning black from the bottom up, and they smelled disgusting.

'Ugh.' Jess looked around her, taking in the vast range built to cook for an army, the huge beams overhead, the massive wooden table and the ancient flagstones on the floor. This kitchen was the size of a normal house. It was fantastic. But right now it was horrid.

Still Raoul seemed bemused. He was thinking of tragedy, Jess thought, whereas right now was the time for thinking of right now. 'You want to open a few windows and doors, Your Highness?' she prodded, moving toward the frying-pan with a handful of dish-cloths and a martial look. 'I'll get rid of this.'

Raoul stared at her for a moment as if he didn't understand—and then crossed to the sink. 'Shove it in here,' he told her.

She raised her brows in incredulity. He really was distracted. 'You're proposing we pour cold water on red-hot cast iron?'

'Well…'

She grinned. 'What do you do in real life, Your Highness? Don't tell me. You're an engineer?'

'I'm a doctor,' he told her and she paused.

'A doctor. A people doctor?'

'That's right.' He frowned, almost as if he was hauling himself back to the here and now. 'Why did you think I might be an engineer?'

That was easy. 'On account of your practicality,' she told him, grinning. 'My cousin's an engineer and he has a four-inch-diameter scar on his shoulder because of just the practicality you're proposing.'

Raoul's brows snapped down in confusion. 'Pardon?'

'Patrick's brilliant,' she told him, folding her dish-cloths into a pad. She was trying not to stare at the way his eyebrows worked when he was confused. It was sort of…sort of very attractive. 'One late night when he was still at university, Patrick got hungry—so he did what any brilliant engineer would do, faced with a can of baked beans and hunger. He heated them on his college-room gas heater. Without opening them. When he finally applied the can opener, the can hit his shoulder and darn near passed straight through.'

Her smile was easier now, less forced. 'And here you are, proposing to stick a red-hot cast-iron pan into cold water. You figure.' She twisted her cloth around the pan and lifted. Doctor or not, prince or not, there was work to be done. 'Open the door,' she ordered. 'Now.'

'Yes, ma'am.' He gave her a bemused look and opened the door.

The cool air of early evening washed in—and smoke rushed out. Jess carried her pan with care straight past Raoul. He stared at her for a minute as if he couldn't work her out.

'Spuds,' she told him, talking back over her shoulder.

'Spuds?'

'You might guess,' she said kindly. 'The little black balls with the disgusting smell.'

He caught himself—he even managed a smile—and he followed. With spuds.

After the smoke-filled kitchen, outside was lovely. A warm sea breeze was drifting across the kitchen garden, and the setting sun was leaving a lingering halo of colour over the distant mountains.

Jess paused on the bottom step and Raoul stopped beside her. Holding his pan.

Hesitating.

This was dumb, Jess thought. It was as if there was some sort of constraining force between them. Something she didn't understand.

Move on, Jess, she told herself firmly. She set her pan down on the stone step and Raoul followed suit. A bunch of hens who looked as if they'd been about to head for the henhouse diverted and gathered round the pots.

Raoul looked at the hens—and then looked back at the pots with indecision.

'These guys will attack these if we leave them here,' he said.

'I guess that's fine,' Jess told him. 'Chooks generally clean off everything edible.'

'Chooks?'

'Australian for hens.' She put on her broadest Australian drawl. 'Chook, chook, chook… It's a much better descriptor than hen, d'ya reckon?'

'Maybe,' he said faintly, sounding stunned. 'Um, the…chooks…aren't going to do so much cleaning as you'd notice. There's not a lot there that's edible.'

'No.' She smiled down at the chickens and said, 'Sorry, guys. I'll give you some toast in a minute to make up for it.'

'We should put them to soak,' Raoul said doubtfully and she sighed and put her hands on her hips.

'Typical male. Of course we should put them to soak. When they're cool. But…did you say Marcel was taking control of this castle in five days?'

'Yes, but—'

'Then I suggest we leave them to soak for, ooh, I'd say about five days,' she said, and she grinned.

He stared at her in something akin to amazement—and then the smile returned.

It was like the sun coming out. It was a killer smile. It made Jess stare up at him and feel something inside twist.

She did not want something inside her to twist.

There was a tentative cluck and a chicken stepped forward toward the pan. It was enough to divert her. Especially as she badly needed to be diverted.

'Don't do it, chook,' she told the bird. 'It's really hot.' She turned to Raoul. 'You say you're a doctor. Have you ever treated chook burns?'

'Um…no.'

'Chooks are pretty dumb,' she said thoughtfully. 'And…you're saying that as of Monday these pans are legally in Marcel's control?'

'For the next eighteen years,' he said. 'Until Edouard turns twenty-one.'

'Hmm. And it's my guess he won't be into counting pots and pans. There's nothing for it, then.' Her smile widened. 'Let's do it.'

She wiped her hands on her skirt in the gesture of a woman preparing for hard work. 'Stand back, all. In the interest of chook health there's nothing else to do.' She walked across to a hose attached to the tap by the back door.

Raoul watched her as if she was something that had appeared on a magic carpet.

'Stand back,' she told him again. 'And whoosh those chooks away.'

'Whoosh?' he asked faintly and her grin deepened.

'Like you did to Marcel,' she told him. 'Only don't whoosh quite so hard.'

There was that smile again. Faint. Just.

She really liked it. They grinned at each other like fools. Then he whooshed the chooks.

She turned on the hose.

It was a very satisfying moment. The jet of cold water, seemingly coming straight from the distant snow-capped mountains, hit the pan with a really satisfactory hiss. The pan erupted in a cloud of steam—

and then there was a solid crack as the cast-iron pan split clean in two.

'Whoops,' Jess said and tried to look contrite. Not very successfully.

Raoul was still looking at her as if she might sprout antennae. 'Whoops?'

'You want to do the spud pan?' she demanded, proffering the hose, and he appeared to collect himself.

'Absolutely,' he told her. He took the hose from her grasp—and pointed.

Crack.

Another pot less for Edouard to inherit.

'How truly satisfying,' Jess said and rubbed her hands on her skirt again—job well done. 'You reckon we could find some more pans to heat up?'

'You're not a designer. You're a demolition expert,' he said on a note of discovery.

'Yep.' She gazed round, considering. 'This is fun. What else can we do here? If Marcel is going to own all this then maybe we could do some real damage.'

'Not fair,' Raoul said, though there was a note at the back of his voice that said he wouldn't mind swinging an axe.

'OK.' She let her demolition work go with reluctance and moved on. 'If we can't demolish, let's eat. But what?' she demanded, returning to the kitchen with purpose. She gazed down at the plates of salad. Delicate. Mouthwatering. Small. 'This won't cut it. I'm hungry.'

'I thought you were an invalid.'

'Invalids need feeding,' she told him. 'Besides, I'm

better. As of now. I'm leaving in the morning.' Then as the lightness faded from his face she regrouped. 'But first, food. Bread. Now. Search.'

'Yes, ma'am.'

She turned her back on him—his look of bemusement was starting to disconcert her—and hauled open the huge refrigerator. That was enough to deflect her thoughts from the man behind her. Or almost. This wasn't a fridge, it was a delicatessen. 'There are six types of cheese in here!' she exclaimed. 'Wow!'

'You're in Alp'Azuri,' he said, still obviously bemused. 'Cheese-making is our speciality.'

'Then the menu is toasted cheese sandwiches,' she declared. 'Followed—I trust—by toast and marmalade. Have you found the marmalade yet?'

'No, I—'

'Then search faster,' she told him with exaggerated patience. 'What sort of prince are you, after all?'

'I have no idea,' he said faintly. 'I have no idea at all.'

It was a really strange meal. They made slabs of cheese sandwiches. They fried them until they were crispy gold, and then they sat at the vast kitchen table and ate them in companionable silence. Raoul continued to be bemused and Jess left him to it. This man had his problems. All she could do was feed him and keep her questions to herself.

Henri appeared just as they finished their second round of sandwiches. He'd come to search for something for Louise to eat. Raoul poured him a glass of wine and then he and Jess combined forces to cook him a mound of sandwiches. They then sent Henri off with another bottle of wine and the toasted sandwiches for Louise and himself to eat in the privacy of her apartments.

'I can't eat with her,' Henri told them but Raoul shook his head. Firmly.

'You're the only one she'll eat with, Henri. You know that. Though whether she'll eat door-stop sandwiches…'

'I suspect she'll love them,' Henri said, looking down at his inelegant pile with a faint smile. 'Ever since we came back here she's been served nothing but five-star cuisine and it gets tiring. I'll tell her that her son made them for her, shall I?'

'She'll never believe you,' Raoul told him. 'But if it'll make her eat them…'

'Certainly tell her that her son made them,' Jess said promptly. 'And tell her that Prince Raoul is also turning out to be a whiz in the washing-up department. There's a cast-iron pot outside, cracked from side to side, with his name on it.'

'Hey, Jess cracked one, too,' Raoul said and they actually giggled in unison—and Henri looked at the pair of them as if they'd taken leave of their senses. But like Raoul, he seemed to have too much on his mind to comment. He left them with his sandwiches and his wine and a bemused smile.

Bemusement seemed to be the order of the day.

'Now for toast and marmalade for us,' Jess said as he left and Raoul looked at her in astonishment.

'I thought you were joking. Where are you putting this?'

'I'm making up for lost time,' she said and then

gave a rueful smile. 'Like your mother, I've been off my food for a bit. Maybe I'll be off my food again tomorrow but for tonight there's toast and marmalade and I refuse to worry.'

He gave her a strange look but asked no questions. They made and ate toast and marmalade. Jess made a couple of extra slices and went out to feed some to the hens, who were standing mournfully around the remains of the pots. They accepted her offering with gratitude and then clucked off to the henhouse.

Raoul watched her all the time, as if stunned.

Did she have two heads? she wondered. She was starting to be really self-conscious here.

What next? she asked herself. What next, besides ignoring the strange looks Raoul was giving her?

With the hens safely locked up for the night, she returned inside and crossed to the sink.

'The servants will cope with the mess in the morning,' Raoul told her but she was already running the water.

'You might be a prince but I'm not. No servant's going to clean up my mess.'

'But…'

'And you've been saying that you're not really a prince,' she told him. She lifted a tea towel and tossed it at him. 'Prove it.'

So she washed and he wiped, once more in silence, and then she drew breath and decided the night had to end.

'Thank you,' she told him. 'This was a great…time out.'

'Time out from what, Jess?' he asked softly, laying

down his tea towel and turning to give her his undivided attention.

She caught herself.

'I mean, time out for you,' she tried. 'Time out from worrying.'

'You were just as in need of time out as I was,' he told her. Then, at her look of confusion, he took her hands in his, lifting them to stare down at her fingers. 'You're what, thirty?'

'Hey! No!' Not quite.

'Close guess?' He smiled.

Close? He was *too* close. He shouldn't smile when he was this close. It was very disconcerting.

What had he asked? It was taking her a lot of trouble to collect enough breath to answer.

'Twenty-nine, if you don't mind,' she managed.

'Twenty-nine. You run a hugely successful design business in Australia. Yet you come here alone, and when you're injured you contact no one and you want no one contacted. No husband?'

'No, I...'

'Parents?'

'Dead.'

'Brothers? Sisters?'

'No.'

'So you're alone in the world.'

'Do you mind?' she said, startled. 'I'm an independent career woman. If we're going to get personal, there are questions I'd like to ask you, too.'

'Like what?'

'Well, you're how old?'

'Thirty-five, but—'

'So why aren't you married? Are you gay?'

'No!' The eyes creased into almost laughter.

'Then—'

'I'm not into marriage,' he told her. 'My parents' marriage was foul and I remember enough of it to steer well clear.'

'Until now. Until Sarah. Do you really think a marriage of convenience would have worked?'

'Of course it would have worked. Why not?'

'And if you met the girl of your dreams?'

'Sarah wouldn't have minded. She probably wouldn't have even known. We'd have done the right thing in public—at least, that was the agreement—but if I met a woman I was attracted to then we'd have a passionate affair until the dream faded.'

She hesitated, strangely chilled. 'Is that right?' she said slowly. 'Until the dream faded. Do dreams always fade?'

'Of course they do,' he told her, almost harshly, and there was that in his face that told her it wasn't just his parents' failed marriage he was basing his life choices on.

'Bad love affair, huh?' she said sympathetically. 'Like me, you dreamed the wrong dream.'

'Hell, Jess…'

'I know. It's none of my business.' She released his hand from hers—almost reluctantly—and faced him square on. She was going nowhere probing further, and she had no right. 'Raoul, I wish you all the best,' she told him. 'I'm really sorry for your troubles, but…it's time I got back to my life and butted out of yours. Thank you for tonight. Thank you for my time out. But I'm going to bed now and I'll leave at first light.'

'Your car's not ready.'

'I'll hire one in the town,' she told him, and smiled. 'You needn't worry. One thing about being successful is that I'm not short of money.' She hesitated. She shouldn't ask more but she really wanted to know. 'And you…you'll go back to Paris?'

'For a while,' he told her. 'Until my mother's settled. I'll try and organise access for her to Edouard. But after that, I'll go back to Africa.'

'Africa?' She sounded astounded. Maybe because she was astounded. 'What are you doing in Africa?'

'I'm a doctor with Médecins Sans Frontières,' he told her. 'I've been working in Somalia for the past three years.'

'You're kidding me.'

'Why should I kid you?'

No reason. No reason at all. Except it required just a bit of readjusting.

'So you'd given up your medicine,' she said slowly, 'to be a prince.'

'If you think I wanted to…' There was a sudden surge of anger, bitten back fast. He hesitated, striving for a reasonable answer to a question he clearly thought was unreasonable. Or a demand on him he clearly thought was unreasonable.

'Jess, this country has been known as one of the most corrupt places in Europe,' he told her, his voice calm again. Logical. But still she could hear the suppressed anger behind the words. 'When Jean-Paul died I had a visit from no less than three heads of state of neighbouring countries. The ordinary citizens here have been bled dry. They've been taxed to the hilt and given nothing in return, so much so that there's the threat of real revolt. The country has become a hotbed of illicit activity with corruption undermining neighbouring stability as well as ours. Change has to occur and it can only change through the constitution—through the ruling prince or regent. And Marcel is appalling. Which was why I was persuaded to marry Sarah and try and do some good. The idea was that I'd come, I'd accept the guardianship of my nephew and leave him with my mother, I'd set in place the changes that have to happen if this country's citizens are not to be exploited—and then I'd leave again.'

'Why?'

'You don't think I want to be a prince?'

'Most people would jump at the chance.'

'I'm not most people,' he said grimly. 'Who was it said that power corrupts and absolute power corrupts absolutely? I watched my father and my brother and I want no part of it.'

'Médecins Sans Frontières is hardly a life career,' she said thoughtfully. 'Doctors Without Borders… They go to the most desperately needy places in the world. I've heard that most people burn out after one or two years. You've been doing it for three?'

'It's not long enough. I'm hardly burned out.'

'Maybe you could stay here and work on the Alp'Azuri medical infrastructure,' she said, and for a fraction of a moment she let her guard slip. 'It's hardly on a par with most western countries. In truth, it's appalling.'

And he got it. He heard the pain of someone speaking from personal experience. She saw the recognition in his eyes. Recognition of tragedy.

'There is that about you,' he said softly, on a note of discovery. 'You're running.'

'I am not running,' she snapped, angry with herself for revealing more than she wanted. 'Any more than you, practising medicine in Somalia when your people need you here.'

'This is not my country. These are not my people.'

'No?'

She took a deep breath. What was she doing? she thought suddenly. What drove this man was nothing to do with her.

'I'm sorry,' she said at last while he stared at her with anger showing clearly on his face. 'OK. This is not your country and you'll be leaving it almost immediately.' She hesitated, trying to find some safer ground. Her perceptions were swinging wildly. This man was a prince. This man was a doctor who fought for lives in third-world countries.

He'd make a wonderful doctor, she thought suddenly and glanced down at his hands. Big, caring, skilled...

Move on, she told herself fiercely. Once again there was that twisting inside that she scarcely understood. She had to find some safe ground.

'And your mother?' she managed. 'What will she do?'

He smiled, albeit faintly. 'My mother has an apartment on the Left Bank. And before you accuse me of deserting her as well as my country, she has Henri.' He saw her look of surprise and explained. 'Henri left the palace when my mother left my father thirty years ago. He's been with my mother ever since, her loyal and devoted servant. Where she goes, Henri goes.'

So all questions were answered. Sort of.

That only left the child, Jess thought. Edouard? Somewhere in this palace there was a three-year-old, a child Jess had never seen.

That was hardly safe ground. She didn't want to see a needful three-year-old, or think about him, or know anything more than she knew already. He was a shadow of trouble and she had no room to cope in her heart with a three-year-old's trouble.

Her heart was devoid of children. Blank. And that was the way it had to stay. Anything else was the way of madness.

Move on.

'Um… Goodnight, then,' she told him, hurriedly, before any other complications could occur.

'Goodnight?' He seemed surprised and maybe that was reasonable. She'd gone straight from inquisition mode to running away.

'Goodnight. Thank you. I'm sorry for your troubles and I'll stop adding to them.'

'You're not adding to anything.'

'Nevertheless I'm leaving. I must.'

She meant to turn away. She meant to turn straight away. But he was watching her and his eyes were suddenly confused. As confused as hers were?

Maybe.

She needed to go.

But still his eyes held hers.

And then, suddenly, she knew what she had to do. It suddenly seemed the right thing to do, the only thing to do.

She-stood on tiptoe and kissed him.

Lightly. Fleetingly.

Why? She hardly knew. It just seemed...appropriate.

It was appropriate.

And more.

The touch of him... It felt right, she thought wonderingly. Kissing this man. Touching this man. Standing in this vast kitchen with the smell of toast and the lingering aroma of burned steak and potatoes... Domesticity was all around them and it made kissing possible. Reasonable. This was a fairy-tale setting, but the toast and the marmalade made it real.

The kiss was real. Because he was real. Raoul was a prince of royal blood but he was a man alone. He was a doctor working where only the bravest went, a man whose country was being destroyed by corruption, an uncle watching his nephew being torn from him. He was a man coping with problems she couldn't bear to think about.

She couldn't help.

'I wish you all the best,' she whispered.

He didn't move. There was a long, drawn-out silence. Too long.

'You'll say goodbye to my mother before you leave?' he asked—heavily—and she nodded.

His hand moved then, his fingers lifting to touch the place on his face where she'd kissed him. It was as though he didn't quite understand what the sensation was.

'Of course I will,' she told him, trying not to watch his fingers. 'I know which her apartments are. I'll say goodbye before I leave in the morning. Thank you, Raoul. For everything.'

She turned to go. And paused.

There was a woman in the doorway.

She was in her late thirties or early forties, Jess thought. She was tall and severely dressed in a nurse's uniform. Her mousy brown hair was hauled severely back into a bun. She stood heavily in the doorway, surveying the couple before her with what seemed dislike.

This wasn't one of the nurses who'd tended her, Jess thought. She hadn't seen this woman before.

But Raoul obviously recognised her. 'Cosette,' he said, sounding surprised. 'How can I help?'

The woman's eyes flicked from Raoul to Jess and back again. Wary. 'I came to tell you I'm leaving,' she told him.

Raoul stilled.

'You're leaving? Now?'

The woman gestured to a cell-phone on her belt. 'The viscount has rung,' she told him. 'He says the whole palace is under his control as of Monday. Including the child. And he's furious. He said you insulted him tonight and he wants everyone out now. All the servants are to leave. If we don't get out now, then we won't have a job on Monday. He's rung everyone. You don't have a staff, Your Highness. I'm sorry.'

And she turned and walked out the back door, leaving them staring after her.

CHAPTER FOUR

'HELL.'

Raoul stood, staring after her as if he'd been struck.

'Um…is this a problem?' Jess asked reluctantly. She wasn't sure whether she wanted to be sucked into this—no, she was *sure* she didn't want to be sucked into this—but the expression on Raoul's face made it impossible for her to walk away.

'Hell,' he murmured again. 'Edouard.'

She had to ask it, although she already knew who they were talking about. The child she'd so carefully avoided thinking of. 'Edouard being your nephew. He's here in the palace?'

'He's here. Cosette has been looking after him.'

She hesitated. 'I thought you said your mother wanted to care for him.'

'My mother…can't. He won't let her. He…' He paused and raked his fingers through his thatch of thick black curls. Despairing. 'You don't understand.'

No, and I don't want to, Jess thought. Go to bed now, she told herself, feeling more desperate by the minute. Leave this mess before it sucks you in.

But—three years old? Alone?

'What do you mean, he won't let her?' It was as if

someone else was speaking, she thought. It was another Jess asking the questions. Not the Jess who'd
walked away from Dom's grave…

'Edouard's been badly neglected,' he was saying.
'And now, for Cosette to walk out just like this…' He
started toward the door. 'Come with me. I need to
check on him straight away.'

But I don't want to, she thought wildly. I can't go
near any needful child.

But Raoul was holding the door for her and waiting
and there was suddenly nothing for it but to pass him
and then walk by his side as he strode swiftly down
the corridors to…

To where?

'My brother had no concept of parenting,' he said,
speaking almost under his breath and striding so
swiftly she almost had to break into a run to keep up
with him. He was explaining to her—but almost
speaking to himself. 'It was no wonder. My father had
no interest and my mother wasn't permitted to interfere. My brother was raised with little affection and
far too much money. He had everything he wanted—
materially—and the end result was that he'd devel-
oped a drug habit by sixteen.'

Jess did a double skip to keep up and glanced across
at his set, angry face.

'Was that how he died?' she asked gently and his
face darkened even further.

'Of course it was,' he said savagely. 'By the time
Jean-Paul was married he was almost off his head. My
father simply didn't care, and it suited the politicians

of this country to have a puppet monarch. While my brother was spaced he didn't interfere with them and that's the way it suited them. The parliament here is made up of men just like Marcel. They vote themselves huge salaries and do nothing. It's been like that for years. Until now.'

'But Edouard…' A little boy. A three-year-old in the middle of this tragedy. Where did he fit in?

'Jean-Paul married a B-grade movie actress whose sole attribute seemed to be the size of her breasts,' he continued, still as if he was speaking to himself. 'She joined right in with the lifestyle Jean-Paul lived. They had Edouard and they handed him over to child-minders. Serial child-minders. Cosette's been with Edouard for six months and that's the longest any-one's been with him. By the time we saw him… He's hardly responding to anyone.'

'Not to your mother?'

'He simply holds himself rigid,' he told her. 'I've watched him. With Cosette he relaxes enough to eat, to sleep, to watch the television he seems to have been put in front of at birth. With anyone else he simply blanks out. Or sobs. My mother spends all the time she can with him but he doesn't respond. And now…' He grimaced. 'Marcel knows the child needs Cosette and he knows my mother will break her heart over a distressed child. She'll do anything to have Cosette stay. Edouard's lost so much already.'

'So he's trying to push you out faster.'

'He's trying to punish us for his treatment tonight.' Raoul's hands were clenching so hard by his sides that

Jess could see the whites of his knuckles beneath his skin. 'Damn him. This will work. My mother will be so distressed that she'll agree to leaving. Cosette will be reinstalled and Edouard will go back to being placed in front of a television every waking minute.'

'And you?' she asked softly. They were climbing stairs now, the grand staircase, and Raoul was taking them three steps at a time. 'You'll go back to Somalia, to your medicine.' She hesitated. 'Raoul, if you'd succeeded in marrying Sarah…what then?'

'I'd have allowed Cosette to stay until Edouard got some sort of link established with my mother,' Raoul snapped. 'Then I'd have asked her to leave. More. I'd have sacked the parliament…'

'Can you do that?'

'I'd have had the constitutional power call a general election,' he told her. 'And I'd have had the power to oversee that it was fair, as no election has been in the history of this country. Marcel's appalling friends would be out on their ear and they know it. But it's not possible.' He reached the top of the stairs and headed left. 'Sarah was our last chance. Now it's over. If Edouard's distraught then there's nothing for it. We'll have to hand over straight away. Give him back his precious Cosette.'

'But how can you do that? Cosette mustn't care too much for him if she's prepared to abandon him as she did tonight.'

'But she'll have him permanently from Monday,' Raoul said savagely. 'Making him suffer for the next few days achieves nothing. Nobody cares about

Edouard and the damnable thing is that there's not one thing I can do about it. You know…' He hesitated, waiting for her to catch up and she had to puff a bit to do so. 'People have pitied me because I've been the second son and didn't stand to inherit the throne. If they only knew.'

He strode on and all she could do was follow.

Finally he paused. At the end of a long corridor there was a pair of baize doors. He hesitated—once more waiting for her to catch up—and then he threw them wide.

'Welcome to hell,' he said enigmatically and stood aside for her to enter.

This, then, was the nursery. It must be a quarter of a mile from the main rooms, Jess thought. It was as far away from the main apartments as it was possible to be. If the little boy's parents had lived in this castle it must have been a ten-minute trek for them to reach him.

Maybe they'd rarely made the trek.

The suite was opulent. That was hardly surprising—everything in this castle was opulent. But this was more than opulent. Some designer somewhere had obviously been given a brief to turn this into a child's fantasy and they'd done just that.

There seemed to be a number of rooms. There was a huge one, the one they'd just entered, with smaller rooms leading off at the side.

The main room was set up as a jungle.

Nothing had been spared. No cost. No flight of imagination. No impingement to copying reality. The setting seemed straight out of Kipling's *Jungle Book*, Jess thought, staring round in incredulity.

There were vast tree trunks—real—and artificial hanging vines. There were stuffed monkeys in the branches. There were snakes slithering down from the trees, stars were painted on the high ceiling, the stars were twinkling through the trees—though dark clouds hovered to the side of the crescent moon as if a giant storm was about to sweep through. Underneath lay a lush green grass-carpet, higher than her ankles.

It was so real that she felt like lifting her feet gingerly in case of snakes.

There was a clearing mid-jungle, where two huge beanbags lay, and here was the only discordant note. In front of the bean-bags was a television. A huge television. And on the screen…

'It's *Extreme Makeover*.' Jess stared at the screen in disbelief as some unfortunate larger-than-life woman was having a knife applied to her fatty abdomen. Liposuction? She closed her eyes and turned away.

'Your nurse and your nephew have been watching *Extreme Makeover*?' she whispered. 'I don't believe it.'

Raoul strode forward and flicked it off. Fast. The fatty abdomen faded to nothing. 'I'd imagine it's just Cosette who's been watching,' he said but his tone was defensive. Maybe justifiably. Maybe she had sounded accusatory.

'So where's Edouard?' she asked. 'If he's not learning how to liposuck.'

He glowered at her.

'Just asking.' She gazed around her in growing anger and decided accusations were well-justified. 'You're a doctor. Maybe you got to watch liposuction at three as well. Maybe that's why you're a doctor now.'

His glower deepened. 'There's no need to get on your high horse. Cosette says he's always sound asleep after six. She says we just disturb him if we come after that. And he gets upset if we come early in the mornings. He sleeps until late.'

'I'll bet he does,' Jess muttered. 'What sort of three-year-old sleeps more than twelve hours at a stretch? None that I know of. So that's why Louise sat with me in the evenings and mornings. She wasn't permitted here. But to be locked out by a servant? You know, if I was a nurse who liked my television, that's what I might tell the family as well. Don't come bothering me in the evenings. Or the mornings. Leave me to do what I want with my charge. Or leave me to watch television while I ignore my charge.'

Raoul's face darkened, as well it might. This was none of her business, Jess told herself. She had no right to vent her anger.

There was no way she could stop herself.

'You must understand that we've come into this as strangers,' Raoul said heavily, defensively. 'Until a month ago we had no contact with Edouard at all. Cosette is his only stability and we've had to respect that.'

'Yeah.' Jess was feeling more and more confused.

She gazed up at the snake above her head. 'I accept that you've been trying—but you have a way to go. Whoever designed this place was sick.'

'It's a nursery.'

'No. It's an adventure playground, great for a brave ten-year-old with playmates and loving parents. But for a three-year-old here on his own… Every time he comes out here he's got a ruddy great boa constrictor hanging over his head, waiting to pounce.'

'Look, maybe I don't like it myself,' Raoul conceded, his tone almost as angry as hers. 'But it's all he knows. When my mother and I came here two weeks ago we talked to a child psychologist. She says it's important he stays with the familiar for as long as possible.'

'That's right,' Jess snapped, and she couldn't keep sarcasm out of her voice. 'Keep to the familiar. Cosette, who watches *Extreme Makeover* while she's child-minding, and boa constrictors waiting to attack at any minute. I don't know who your psychologist was but I beg to disagree.'

'Look, who are you to—?'

She wasn't going there. 'I'm no one,' she snapped. 'No one at all. If you knew how much I didn't want to do this…' She took a deep breath. 'Where is he?'

'He'll be asleep.' He motioned to the door on the left and Jess turned.

But she hesitated.

There was a part of her—a really big part—that was screaming not to go any further.

But there was a child through this door who was

three years old. Three. Orphaned. Alone. With boa constrictors for company and *Extreme Makeover* on television and a child psychologist with rocks in her head.

Maybe Raoul was right, she told herself desperately. Maybe the psychologist was right. She'd walk in there and he'd be asleep. Peacefully. Everything would be fine. He'd be stronger than she had imagined.

OK, so go in there, she told herself. Don't hesitate. She could see for herself that he was fine, she could ease her stupid qualms, and tomorrow she could leave. The worst thing that could happen here was that Raoul and his mother would have to cope with a distraught child for a few days. Cosette would take over next Monday and things would settle for this child as they'd been settled since he was born.

The child had nothing to do with her.

She glanced again at Raoul. His face was a mix of anger and doubt.

Doubt?

He was as unsure as she was, she thought.

It was enough. Before she could go any further down the introspection path—which was getting her exactly nowhere—she walked across to open the bedroom door.

There was a nightlight in the corner, lighting the room enough to see.

Edouard wasn't asleep at all.

The little boy was curled tightly in the far corner

of his too-big bed. His eyes were wide and wakeful. He was all eyes, she thought. All scared eyes.

He was as fair as his big uncle was dark, with wispy white-blond curls, skin that was almost translucent and huge brown eyes that all but enveloped his tiny face. He lay staring at the open door, his face tight with anxiety.

Why wouldn't you be anxious in this bed? Jess thought, stunned at what she saw. The boa constrictor had triggered her anger and this scene was doing nothing to calm it.

The little boy's bed was a bed built for a crown prince, not for a baby, and he took up about two per cent of it. There was not a toy in sight. The starched white top sheet was stretched tightly over his chin—there was miles of sheeting, stretched so tight it almost seemed to cut into his chin. The royal insignia was embroidered on the side of the sheet, making the little boy seem even more insignificant. The bed was made with hospital corners, not a crease in sight.

He lay rigid and expressionless. As Jess took a tentative step toward him, he flinched.

Three-year-olds didn't flinch, Jess thought in incredulity. Unless…maybe someone had yelled. She glanced out through the jungle to the television and a likely scenario presented itself: You be quiet or else.

She was being fanciful.

But she watched the terror grow in these huge brown eyes and she knew she wasn't being fanciful at all. This child was nowhere near sleep. He was wide awake but the lack of creases in the bedclothes said that he hadn't moved a muscle in the crazy, too-big bed since he'd been put there.

Since when? Six o'clock was his bedtime, Raoul had said. Three hours ago?

Raoul had walked in behind her. The child's eyes moved past Jess to his uncle, and to her relief there was a faint lessening of the terror. It was as if he already knew that when this man was around he wouldn't be yelled at.

'You're not asleep,' Raoul said softly. 'Hi, Edouard. This is Jessie.'

No response.

'Pick him up,' Jess urged. 'Oh, for heaven's sake, he looks terrified.'

'If I pick him up he cries,' Raoul told her. 'The same with my mother.'

'So what does he do when you don't pick him up?' she snapped. 'Does Cosette pick him up?'

'Sure she does.'

'Does she cuddle him? Have you seen her?'

'No, but—'

'Have you seen her take him outside?' she demanded. 'Have you seen her play with him?'

'He has his schedule. We don't interfere.'

Jess took a deep breath. Another. She should get out of here. She should run.

Edouard's eyes were on her face again. Watchful. Filled with apprehension.

He was thinking that she was yet another babysitter, she thought. Another servant paid to look after him.

She stared down at him in dismay. His hair was just like…

No.

But right then, right as she made the comparison, she knew it was too late. There'd been a connection and she couldn't break it now.

She walked forward and scooped the little boy out of his bed, mussing his bedclothes in the process. Ignoring the way his body turned rigid. Ignoring the tension that said he was about to open his mouth and wail.

He was thin, she thought. Far too thin. He was dressed in rich-red pyjamas, with that crazy insignia on the jacket. Ridiculous.

She hauled him against her breast. He jerked back, ramrod stiff, and his eyes moved frantically. He opened his mouth, prepared to wail.

'Hey, it's OK, Edouard,' she whispered and she plonked herself down on the crazy, too-big bed. She placed her finger on his lips. 'You're not to cry. There's no need.' She looked up at Raoul. 'You know Raoul. You know your uncle. I'm his friend, Jess.'

'Cosette,' he whispered, his bottom lip quivering in fear. 'I want Cosette.'

'Cosette had to leave in a hurry,' she told him and her arms held him close. Stiff or not, she held him hard against her body, imparting warmth. 'But that's all right because your uncle Raoul's here and he's your family. Your grandma's here, too. Shall I call her?'

The eyes didn't register a thing.

'Do you have a teddy?' she demanded and once more there was no expression at all. The child's eyes said he was expecting nothing. Any minute he might cry but even that required emotion he wasn't sure he was prepared to commit.

'He's got so many stuffed toys I can't count,' Raoul said ruefully. He motioned out to the jungle, where monkeys, elephants, giraffes, snakes, every imaginable stuffed toy was set up in among the carefully orchestrated décor.

'I don't mean decorations,' Jess said scornfully. 'I mean a teddy. A friend. I know exactly who you need.' She looked up at Raoul. 'Uncle Raoul, we need an adventure leader,' she told him. 'Edouard's not the least bit ready to go to sleep, are you, Edouard?'

There was just the faintest, almost imperceptible shake of a blond head. His lips were still quivering, but clearly anything might prove better than lying in this bed.

'OK. I have a sore shoulder and your uncle Raoul is very strong,' Jess told him. 'Raoul, your nephew needs a piggyback.'

'A piggyback,' Raoul said, as if she might be losing her mind.

'Turn around,' she ordered. She stood up, still holding Edouard close. 'Edouard, do you know what a piggyback is?'

Another shake of the head, more definite this time.

'Just think of your uncle Raoul as a two-legged horse,' she told him. 'I put you on his back—like this.' She swung him against Raoul's broad back. 'You hang on round his neck as hard as you can. Uncle Raoul will hold you underneath. Raoul,' she ordered, 'hang on to Edouard underneath.'

'Yes, ma'am,' Raoul told her and hung on to Edouard underneath.

But Edouard didn't hang on. He pulled back, fearful.

'I don't want to,' he whispered.

'You know, your uncle Raoul makes a very good horse,' Jess told him, deliberately misunderstanding his fear. 'And you don't want to go to sleep yet, do you?'

'N...no.' An almost inaudible whisper.

'Well, then.' She wasn't taking no for an answer. She simply wound his tiny arms around his uncle's neck and then she stepped back.

He hung on.

'Excellent,' she told them both. 'Follow me.'

'Where to?' Raoul asked.

'It's an adventure,' she told him. 'We're off to meet a bear. A little bear. A friend bear for Edouard.' She took a deep breath and tried to swallow pain. 'Someone who...someone who needs Edouard as much as Edouard needs him. Ready?'

'Yes, ma'am.'

'Then gee-up,' she told him. 'Pronto.' She led the way, glancing at the jungle with repugnance as she passed through. 'We'll get those snakes out of these trees before you come back here,' she told Edouard as Raoul had to duck to avoid a couple of particularly long and vicious fangs. 'Things are going to change. You wait and see. Just follow.'

And she took off down the corridor, leaving two very confused princes to follow.

She took them to her apartment.

Edouard didn't say a word the whole way and neither did Raoul. It was as if they were both stunned.

In truth, so was Jess. What she was doing seemed crazy, but she no longer had a choice. If she walked away she'd regret it and she already had enough regrets to last a lifetime.

Her apartments were better than Edouard's, she decided when they reached her rooms. Sure, her rooms were still opulent but they were much more cheerful. The nursery must have been warmed by some form of central heating. Here there was a fire in the grate. Jess had lain on the bed this afternoon and the covers were rumpled and cushions were scattered. There were magazines on the floor and Louise had put a vase of random, cottage-type flowers in a vase by her bed.

After Edouard's decorator nursery, this looked almost homey.

She led them into her bedroom. 'Take a seat,' she told Raoul and he sat on the bed, gingerly, with Edouard still clutched firmly to his neck.

'You're stopped,' she told them kindly. 'You can readjust. It gets pretty uncomfortable to keep piggy-backing in the sitting position. Edouard's allowed to sit on your lap now.'

'My lap?' Raoul said, sounding French, and Jess grinned.

'Your knee. I guess princes of the blood don't have laps. Edouard, would you like some lemonade?'

Edouard looked astounded.

'We'll all have lemonade,' she decreed. There was a small refrigerator in her sitting room. She went out and poured three glasses of lemonade and returned to find Edouard sitting on Raoul's...knee.

They both looked so apprehensive that she giggled.

'Hey, I don't bite,' she said and handed over the glasses.

Edouard stared into his glass in absolute suspicion.

'There are bubbles?' he whispered and there was another shock. A royal prince reaching three years old without meeting lemonade?

'Sure there are bubbles,' she said, trying not to get choked up. 'They tickle your nose. Try it.'

Edouard glanced at his uncle. Raoul smiled and drank some of his.

Edouard stared at Jess, who drank some of hers.

He hesitated—and then he took a sip.

His eyes widened. He took another sip. And another.

It had been a test, Jess thought, letting breath out that she didn't know she'd been holding. And they'd just passed.

'I like it,' he said, on a long note of discovery, and Jess grinned.

'Me, too. What about you, Uncle Raoul?'

'Me, too,' he said definitely and he smiled—and

suddenly they were grinning at each other like fools again, and that crazy twist inside her that she'd been trying to put aside all evening slammed back so hard that her breathing got tricky.

She wasn't sure how to manage this breathing business. What was going on?

'Um…teddy,' she managed, but Raoul was still smiling at her and it took all the strength she possessed to break contact.

'Teddy?' he said, softly, almost wonderingly, and she knew that whatever was twisting her insides was having a similar effect on him.

She ignored it. Or she tried to ignore it. She walked over to the wardrobe where her suitcase lay stored in its cavernous depths. She knew exactly where Teddy was. In a moment she had him out, and was walking back to the bed.

Dammit, she wasn't going to cry. She wasn't.

She reached the bed, and she held out one small bear.

'Edouard, this is Sebastian,' she told him. She crouched down so her eyes were on a level with Edouard's. Raoul had him on his knee so she was almost touching his legs. It was a crazily intimate setting. But then, it was a crazily intimate gesture.

It might not work. It might be stupid. What made her think so strongly that it was the right thing to do? That Dom would have wanted this…?

'Edouard, Sebastian is a very old bear,' she told him. 'He was my bear when I was a little girl, and then he belonged to a little boy called Dominic.

Dominic can't look after him any more, and for the past few weeks he's been sitting in the bottom of my suitcase. But that's a very sad place for a special bear to be. He's been lonely and he badly wants a friend. Would you like Sebastian, Edouard?'

Edouard considered. His small face was intent, as if knowing instinctively that this was a very serious charge.

Sebastian lay in Jess's hands. He'd been patched and re-patched. His eyes didn't quite match. His nose was fraying, and one leg was very much shorter than the other. He gazed out at the world with world-weary, crooked eyes and a crooked little smile that had been stitched and re-stitched but had never stopped smiling in all the years of his life.

He was one special bear.

Jess held him out, and she felt her gut wrench as she did so. But it felt right. It felt…fine.

She looked up into Edouard's face and she saw the intent look he was giving Sebastian and she thought, yep, here was his home.

'He looks sad,' Edouard said even though the little bear was smiling.

'He's been in the bottom of a suitcase in my cupboard,' Jess told him. 'He's been very lonely. He needs a friend.'

'Sebastian needs me?' His voice was too old for his years, Jess thought, and more and more she knew this was the right thing to do.

'I guess he does,' she told him and waited while

Edouard considered some more. Finally, he reached out a finger and touched the ragged nose.

Then very carefully, as if Sebastian might break at any minute, he accepted him into his hold. He held him at arm's length for a long minute—and then hauled him in closer. Protectively.

'He doesn't have any clothes,' he whispered. 'He's sad because he doesn't have anything to wear.'

'Do you think so?' Raoul was smiling. She noticed his smile, and even more she thought, this felt good. Very good. And not just for Edouard. The wash of grey fog she'd been living in for the last few months had lifted. Just a bit. Just a fraction, like the sun glimmering out from the clouds, but the sun was on her face and she felt, for this magic moment, a shard of glorious freedom. And she intended to pursue it for all it was worth.

'We could make him some trousers,' she said, and her two princes looked puzzled.

'Now?' Edouard whispered and she nodded.

'Now.'

'How?' Raoul demanded, surprised out of his sideline role.

She smiled. 'Magic. Watch.' She disappeared back to her wardrobe, to her suitcase, then returned carrying a frame—a tiny loom already threaded with black warp thread. She also carried a handful of brightly coloured balls.

'We'll start from the ground up,' she told the boys. 'I have this set up so I can try out various yarns for effect. Raoul, set Edouard down. There's work to be done.'

She dropped her balls at her feet and skeins of brightly coloured yarn rolled over the imperial carpet. These were amazing skeins, carefully collected from one producer, each one sourced and labelled. At this one place Jess had visited before her accident she'd known she'd been right to come. Alp'Azuri was a weaver's paradise.

The balls were unique, vibrant colours and amazing textures. Magic. She'd produced only the coarser of her selection—there was no time for fine weaving now—but the coarser ones were magic enough.

She knelt on the carpet, setting her frame on the floor.

'I need you to choose four skeins for the cross thread—the weft,' she told the boys. 'If we're to do trousers tonight we can't work with any more. Edouard, can you count to four?'

Edouard was clutching Sebastian tightly. He climbed down from Raoul's lap and he held up four fingers.

'Un, deux, trois, quatre.'

Jess beamed. This tiny man-child was turning more and more into a child as she watched. 'I usually say one, two, three, four because I'm Australian,' she told him. 'Sebastian is Australian, too. But he's a fast learner. I bet you he understands you right now. OK, choose...what do you say? *Un, deux, trois, quatre* balls so we can make cloth for Sebastian's trousers.'

'Wouldn't it be easier if we cut up a sheet or something?' Raoul ventured and he was given a pitying look for his pains.

'Trousers? From a sheet? Would you wear trousers made from a sheet?'

'Maybe not,' he said faintly and she grinned.

'There you go, then. Sebastian deserves splendid trousers and that's what we'll make him. All hands on deck.'

'I don't understand all hands on deck,' Edouard complained and she grinned still more.

'It means I'm the captain and I'm saying we have work to do. I've never had two princes to boss around before but I'm bossing now. Work. Now.'

'Yes, ma'am,' Raoul told her and she smiled up at him.

Damn, there was that gut-twisting sensation that was threatening to spiral out of control.

She had work to do.

She couldn't keep smiling at Raoul forever.

No matter how much she wanted to.

CHAPTER FIVE

WHAT followed was a truly excellent hour.

Jess's fingers were true weaver's fingers. Edouard chose his yarns: red, gold, a deep blue and a soft lemon that made her smile. She attached the threads, she considered for a little, and then she set to work. The shuttles flew in her hands, back, forth, pressing each thread into place in her chosen pattern while the boys looked on in wonder.

Edouard watched for a few minutes and after a bit she asked him if he'd like to place the shuttles for her. To her surprise his fingers were nimble and sure, and he seemed to sense the pattern she was working without being told. She'd want a thread and his fingers were already reaching for the right shuttle.

This little boy was intelligent and he was fascinated. As was Raoul. She had his undivided attention. It made her feel strange, but the shimmer of joy was still with her. The grey that had been with her since Dom's death was held at bay by their absorption.

She worked fast, and in half an hour there was a good half a yard of cloth; enough for any bear's trousers.

'Now what?' Raoul said faintly as she drew the

cloth from her frame and gazed at it, considering. 'It's beautiful. We should frame it.'

'Frame it? When it can be useful?' That was what she'd been doing with Sebastian himself, she thought, her joy fading a little. She'd been shoving the little bear down the bottom of her suitcase. Unable to cope with holding him, unable to look at him but also unable to let go. Holding him in store for when he could be useful.

Like now.

'What is it, Jess?' Raoul asked, and she hauled herself out of her introspection and made herself focus.

'Nothing,' she said abruptly, reaching for scissors. 'There'll be no more framing. This might be a pretty piece of cloth but Sebastian needs trousers.'

It was a very rough pair of trousers. She had no sewing machine and Edouard was starting to droop, but she badly wanted the trousers to be finished tonight. So she cut a front and a back and sewed them together swiftly with a neat, fast backstitch, using a rough blanket stitch to stop fraying. She turned the band at the waist, plaited the remainder of the skeins and threaded the resulting cord through the band. She deliberately released threads at the hems to give the trousers a Robinson Crusoe look, and Sebastian's trousers were complete.

'There.' She held them up for inspection. 'What do you think?'

They were all still sitting on the floor. Edouard was back on Raoul's lap—whoops—knee. He was fighting weariness but there was no way he'd sleep while his Sebastian was being clothed.

Jess held out the trousers and he accepted them as a man might accept a piece of priceless artwork. He looked doubtfully up at Raoul. Raoul smiled. He took a deep breath, and then he started pulling the trousers onto his bear.

Two heads, one dark, one fair, bent over the teddy while Jess looked on and fought back another stupid urge to cry.

'They fit,' Edouard said in a voice of wonder and Raoul smiled down at the teddy and touched Sebastian's nose as Edouard himself had done.

'How could you doubt they would fit?' he demanded of his nephew. 'We have a master weaver and seamstress in our midst. A wonder weaver. Our Jess.'

Our Jess. Damn, there were the tears again.

She wasn't going to cry. She wasn't.

'Can I take him to bed?' Edouard asked, and there was a sudden quaver in his voice. Bed. He'd had time out, his voice said. Now he had to face his too-big bed again—and his jungle.

And it was out before she could help herself. 'Would you like to sleep here?'

What was she doing? How could she have asked it? She felt the colour drain from her face as she said the words, and Raoul's eyes snapped down in confusion.

'In your bed?' Edouard whispered, and it was too late to back out.

'Yes.' She swallowed. 'Just for tonight.'

Edouard looked through to Jess's big bedroom. The light was off but there a fire was lit in there as well, making the room look incredibly appealing. It seemed a million miles from his horrible nursery.

'Yes, please,' Edouard whispered—and then there was nothing to do but to watch as Raoul prepared his little nephew for bed.

She stared into the flames while he carried him through to the bathroom. She stared at some more flames while he settled him into Jess's bed. He tucked Edouard between the sheets—and tucked Sebastian-Bear between the sheets as well.

The flames were riveting. She wouldn't watch—she couldn't—as Raoul kissed his nephew goodnight and then stroked his fair curls until the wide eyes drooped and he drifted into sleep.

When Raoul finally turned away, Jess was still crouched on the floor, surrounded by the remains of her weaving and her trouser-making. She was staring at her flames as if she was trying to remember every flicker.

She didn't say a word. She couldn't.

Finally Raoul sank into the floor beside her, as if he'd come to some major decision.

'I think it's time you told me, Jess,' he said softly.

'Told me?'

'Start with Sebastian-Bear,' he said gently, and he lifted her hand. 'Sebastian belonged to you. Now he belongs to Edouard. But there was someone in the middle. Your child? Tell me who, Jess.'

'Dominic.'

How could it hurt to say the word? she thought. It was a magical little name. She'd always loved it. She loved it still.

'Dominic was your son?' he asked, still in the soft, half-whisper that the firelight seemed to encourage. He'd flicked down the power of the overhead light as he'd returned to her, so the light was kind; a soft dusk of flickering firelight that hid the distress on her face. Or she hoped it hid the distress. He was acute, this man. He saw…

'Dominic was my son,' she whispered. 'He died three months ago.'

'How old?'

'He was four.' Four years, two days. He'd celebrated his fourth birthday.

Just.

'How did he die?'

'Leukaemia,' Jess told him, her voice growing mechanical now. Dull. 'He was ill for almost two years. I fought so hard, and so did he. He had every treatment possible. I tried everything.'

'I'm so sorry.'

'Tragedies happen,' she said wearily. 'You move on.'

'Do you?'

Silence. The fire crackled and hissed, absorbing pain.

'*You* tried so hard,' Raoul said at last, speaking slowly, as if absorbing every thought. 'And *Dominic* fought. You don't mention Dominic's father.'

'Warren didn't like illness.' This was easier, she

thought thankfully. Talking about Warren was like talking about…nothing. 'He left us a month after Dominic was diagnosed. By the time Dominic died, Warren had a new wife and a baby daughter. He didn't even come to the funeral.'

Raoul's face stilled, appalled. 'Tough,' he whispered and she shook her head.

'Warren wasn't tough,' she told him. 'He was weak. Not like his son. Dominic was just the bravest…'

She stopped. There was a long pause, broken only by the sound of the fire.

'So you've come here to try and recuperate,' he said at last, and she flinched.

'You don't recuperate from a child's death,' she whispered, and she couldn't stop the sudden flash of anger. 'But that's what they all said. You go overseas and forget, they told me. Start again. How can I start again? Why would I want to?'

'Like me,' he said softly and her eyes flew to his. 'Only harder.'

'What…what do you mean?'

'I believed them,' he told her, his voice gentling. 'Or maybe, like you, they just wore me down by repeating their mantra and I hoped like hell they were right.'

She paused. The fire died down a little. It was crazily intimate; crazily close. It was as if the world had stopped, paused, giving them a tiny cocoon of unreality. Space in the face of shared tragedy.

'You've lost someone, too?' she whispered, though she already knew the answer.

'My twin. My sister. Lisle.'

His twin sister. She stared at his face and she saw the bleakness of loss.

'How long ago?'

'Three years.' He shrugged. 'I know. I should be over it.'

'Of course you shouldn't be over it,' she snapped. She stared some more into his strained face. 'I guessed it,' she said, savagely, angry at herself for not letting the thought surface before. 'I knew.'

'How?'

'It's a look,' she told him. 'I saw it in the hospital. I saw it in the faces of those who knew there was no longer hope. It's an emptiness, a hole. You and your mother... Jean-Paul's death has hurt, but it's also brought back Lisle's death.'

'I don't have an emptiness,' he said but she shook her head.

'No? Then why Médecins Sans Frontières?'

'I just... It seemed the right thing to do, to be a doctor.' He hesitated but the firelight was enough to encourage him to go on. It was like the confessional, Jess thought. This night there were no secrets. 'Lisle was deprived of oxygen during birth,' he told her. 'She had cerebral palsy. She was so bright, so damned intelligent, and her body was a prison.'

He paused for a moment and she thought he'd stop. But she didn't speak. She simply waited.

'That's why my mother left my father,' he told her. 'As soon as my father realised Lisle would be disabled, he demanded she be placed in an institution. Of course, my mother refused. We had servants here to help with Lisle's physical needs, and Lisle was as intelligent as any of us. She loved us. To do anything but keep her as an integral part of our family seemed unthinkable. But physical disability horrified my father and he insisted. Mama fought him—she held out for six long years. But then it was time for schooling, and there were to be no tutors here. My father refused to have them. And he started being cruel to Lisle. So Mama had a choice and it was a hellish one. Place Lisle into an institution, or walk away from the palace. There was no way my father would release his grip on his heir so that also meant walking away from my brother.'

'Oh, no. Oh, Raoul.'

'It broke her heart,' Raoul said bitterly. 'Jean-Paul was twelve. She'd hoped she could maintain access—she'd hoped that Jean-Paul himself could understand her decision, but of course he couldn't. He hated her for leaving. And my father... I think my father just dismissed her. She was forgotten the moment she walked out of the palace and she was never permitted back.'

To make a choice between her children... Jess's heart recoiled in horror. 'I can't imagine how she can have managed.'

'Oh, she managed,' Raoul said and a hint of a remembering smile played across his lips as he left the tragedy of his childhood and moved on. 'She took Lisle and me to Paris. She raised us with love, and she tried not to let the tragedy of leaving her eldest child spoil our childhood. No one answered our phone calls to the palace but we wrote to Jean-Paul every week. Every one of us did. But he never answered. Mama thought for a long while that my father was keeping the letters from him, but no. The servants confirmed for us…Jean-Paul, like my father, had simply moved on.'

'And Lisle?' Jess asked, and his face softened. Pleasure returning.

'Lisle ended up with a first-class university degree,' he told her. 'She loved life. She had friends, she had the best sense of humour… We were so proud of her. She was a truly wonderful person.'

'But she died.'

The smile faded. 'In the end her body defeated her,' he said softly. 'She suffered infection after infection and finally we couldn't save her.'

He fell silent, and she saw the pain etched across his face. There was a part of her—a really big part of her—that wanted to reach out and touch him. No. But it took an almost superhuman effort to keep her hands to herself.

'As I said, that was three years ago,' he continued and maybe he didn't sense what she was thinking. He was staring into the firelight—not at her. 'I was already a practising doctor and I thought, after watching the courage with which Lisle faced life, that the least I could do was try to help others. And, of course, everyone said I should get away and forget.'

'Hence Médecins Sans Frontières?'

'Mm.'

'Hence the scar?' she asked, wanting suddenly to reach out—to trace its course. She did no such thing.

'Tribesmen involved in a who-gets-the-doctor-first dispute,' he said, smiling faintly. 'I tried to referee and then there were three of us needing attention.'

She couldn't touch it. She musn't.

'And now you're back here,' she said softly, gripping her hands firmly into place; staring at the firelight and not looking at him. 'You're trying to save your country. And your mother is facing losing again. Losing her grandson. Walking away.'

'It's damnable,' he told her. He glanced through the door to the bed, where Edouard lay clutching his Sebastian in sleep. 'He's so…desperate. You know, in the weeks we've been here my mother has given him toys but he's not looked at anything. Tonight has been magic.' He hesitated, and she saw him form the question she knew had to come. 'Sebastian is Dominic's teddy?'

'He's Edouard's teddy,' she told him, her voice firming.

'But…'

'Edouard needs him now.' She was speaking more firmly than she felt, but she knew this was right. 'We move on, Raoul. We both need to move on. We need to remember Lisle and Dominic—but we also need to get on with our lives.'

'Easier to say than do.'

'It's not so hard. You just have to be definite. You just have to remember toast and marmalade makes you feel good.'

'And firelight,' he told her. 'And making trousers for teddies.'

'That too,' she told him. She stared at him then, straight at him. There was such trouble in his face, she thought. She was coping with the loss of her child, but she wasn't alone in her grief. This man was not only coping with the death of his twin and the more recent death of his brother, but he was also facing his mother's sorrow. And in the next room, in her bed, was a little boy who would be raised alone because this man had fought and lost.

'Why did you never marry?' she asked for the second time, gently into the night. 'Until now?'

It was a presumptuous question but it seemed tonight that nothing was presumptuous. For this night, for this time, there were no barriers.

'I hardly thought of it,' he told her. 'I guess... Lisle's health was so precarious and she needed so much help that there never seemed time to get heavily involved outside our family circle.'

He smiled then. It was a mere echo of the smile she loved so much but it was a smile for all that. 'But I haven't exactly been puritanical,' he told her. 'If you think I've led a life of pure hard work and no fun...'

'Women, eh?' she said, following the lead he was giving with his smile, and magically, wonderfully, he grinned. 'Lots of women?'

'A thousand at least,' he told her, and she smiled straight back at him.

'Excellent.' She hesitated. 'So...you've had a thousand-odd women but when you needed to marry there was only Sarah to choose? A relative who—from my point of view anyway—maybe didn't seem the wisest choice.'

'She seemed a good choice,' he told her, and his voice was suddenly stiff again. Defensive. 'I didn't want to be held down.'

'Right,' she said drily. 'Well, she's surely not holding you down. And now what? If Sarah was a business proposition, can you not make another? Can't you find another good choice by Monday? Another bride who'll not keep you from your thousand other women?'

'I was joking.'

'I know you were joking,' she told him. 'But there must be someone. Maybe you could advertise.'

'Oh, sure,' he said, self-mockingly. 'I should just put a notice up on the main palace gate. Wanted, one princess.'

'Why not? You'd be swamped.'

'By women who'd expect something. By a woman I didn't know, who could lead to all sorts of complications. It's impossible. The woman I want would have to marry and then step away. Sarah was doing it for money and prestige, but she knew enough of the rules of the monarchy to toe the line. Or I thought she did. And she didn't mind the goldfish bowl she was stepping into. She'd have enjoyed the attention of the Press. Anyone else it'd swamp.'

Silence. More silence.

The fire crackled and Jess suddenly felt dizzy. She

put a hand down onto the thick Persian rug she was kneeling on—as if she needed to steady herself.

She did need to steady herself.

Something was forming in the back of her mind. Something so preposterous it was taking her breath away.

Could she?

How could she not?

'Unless…unless your bride didn't live here,' she said, softly, sounding the idea out in her head as the idea formed. 'Unless she lived somewhere like… Australia? There'd be no media if your bride packed and left for Australia the moment the ceremony was ended.'

There was a moment's stunned silence. Raoul's face stilled.

The world seemed to hold its breath.

'What are you suggesting?' he asked at last, but he knew. Of course he knew, and it was too late to back out now.

And she didn't want to back out. She glanced through to the bedroom. This wasn't a big thing, she thought. She could do this. She had her life and she could get on with it regardless. A mere marriage would make no difference to her.

And it was a positive thing to do. A definite action. It was like making toast and marmalade, but the slivers of lightness of this action wouldn't just be for her. By her actions Edouard could be made safe.

'I'm saying that your answer could be right here,' she said softly. 'I'm saying I'll marry you.'

'You...'

'On terms,' she said hurriedly. 'On very definite terms.'

On terms.

Raoul stared at the girl beside him. She was staring into the flames, as if the thing she'd just said was an aside; of no importance.

It was as if she'd said, If you'd like, I'll make you a cup of tea, instead of, If you'd like, I'll marry you.

'What are you saying?' he asked at last and she even smiled.

'Hey, it's no big deal. You're obviously desperate for a wife. I've ditched my spineless husband, who I married when I was too young to know better, and I'm available.' Something occurred to her then, and her brow wrinkled into a furrow. She looked absurdly young, he thought. She was dressed for dinner, her clothes were lovely, but her freckles and her snub nose and her close-cropped curls still made her seem about seventeen. Only she wasn't seventeen. There was a depth of world knowledge behind her eyes that more than matched his own. While he'd been fighting for his sister's life, and for unknown lives in Somalia, she'd been fighting for the life of her tiny son, and who was to say which had taken the worst toll?

'Um... But I've suddenly thought,' she said and she did turn and look at him then, 'there's no rule that you marry another princess or someone royal, is there?'

'No, but...'

Her brow wrinkled further. 'Or a virgin? That'd be a worry.'

'Not a virgin,' he told her and the relief on her face made him smile. 'I had planned to marry Sarah. She'd been married before.'

'There you go, then,' she said as if all problems were solved. 'Job's done.'

'But you don't want to marry me,' he managed and she raised her brows in mock-surprise.

'You don't think so? I don't see why not. You're very handsome.'

'Gee, thanks.'

She giggled. It was an amazing sound, he thought. When had he last heard a woman giggle?

'Close your mouth,' she said kindly. 'Stop looking hornswoggled.'

'Hornswoggled?'

'I'm not sure of the translation,' she told him. 'Maybe it's ''you could have knocked me over with a porrywiggle''.'

'I don't think I even want to go there,' he said faintly. 'Jess, have you any idea what you're offering?'

'Yes—and it's a really serious offer,' she told him, and coloured. 'I know it's unusual—Australian dress designer proposes to Prince Regent of Alp'Azuri—but then the situation is unusual.'

'But...'

'But nothing. You know I don't want anything of you,' she told him, talking hurriedly before he could speak. As though she was fearful he was reaching all the wrong conclusions. 'I accept that you can't advertise for a bride because you might get crazy people and there's no time to vet them, and of course there's no time to vet me. You'd have to take me at my word. I don't want to be a princess. I don't want money— my business is going very nicely, thank you—and I don't want fame. My proposition is that I'll marry you, I'll see Edouard safe and then I'll disappear back to Australia. I'll be a one-day wonder for the media. Back home my staff can protect me from intrusion, and you can get on with ruling this country as it ought to be ruled.'

She hesitated again and then said, more than a little self-consciously, 'You know, I do understand your qualms. But you needn't have them. As I don't have qualms about you. I haven't known you for long, but I've known you for long enough to accept that you'd make a fairer ruler of this country than Marcel ever would. And…' she glanced through into the bedroom '…you'd make a far nicer guardian for Edouard.'

'Jess…' He could hardly think of how to respond, but once again she stopped him.

'It could work,' she said, urgently now. 'Don't knock me back without thinking about it. I know the last thing you want is an unroyal bride—what would they call me, a commoner?—but it could work.'

It could.

His mind shifted into overdrive. Marry Jess.

He could marry Jess, quietly, swiftly. He could retain rights over this realm.

He'd never wanted this. From the time his mother had taken him and Lisle away from this palace when he was aged six, he hadn't looked back. There'd been so much hurt. Even as he grew older he'd refused to think of himself as royal. He'd thrown himself into his medical career and he loved it.

But now…the last few weeks had shown what desperate straits this little country was in. Until Jean-Paul's death he'd blocked it out—he hadn't wanted to know what he could do nothing about. But the mess the country was in was now obvious even to outsiders and the moment he'd arrived here it threatened to overwhelm him. On the surface the country was a wonderful little tourist mecca, but scratch the surface and there was grinding poverty on every level.

He could install a decent government, he thought. This was what he'd planned when he'd talked Sarah into marriage. He could set up a decent infrastructure, install a government that would work, and then he could return again to the medicine and the obscurity that he…

'You see, there's my condition,' she said, apologetically, as though she was reading his thoughts, and to his amazement it seemed she had been. 'I'm not prepared to let you do that.'

'Do what?'

'Dump it on your mother.'

'I beg your pardon?'

'That's what you planned,' she said, and as well as apologetic she sounded defensive. 'I know you'll organise a better government here and things will be better for the country. But your mother's not strong enough to cope with a little boy and you know it.'

'She'll have servants,' he said, stunned, and Jess winced.

'Edouard doesn't need servants. He needs you.'

'I don't do family.'

'Of course you do,' she told him, as though he was being thick. 'Oh, I know, you had to walk away from your father and your brother when you were six and that must have been appalling. And then you lost Lisle, which broke your heart. But right over there...' She motioned to her bed. 'Over there you have Edouard. He's your family, whether you want it or not. He doesn't want servants. He doesn't want designer nurseries or money or anything you can organise from a distance while you're off saving the world in Somalia. There's a world here to save. I hate to say this, Your Highness. It's absolutely none of my business, but your country needs you, your mother needs you, your nephew needs you, and your place while Edouard is growing up is right here.'

There was a long silence. A stunned silence. He stared at this chit of a girl and she stared right back. Not flinching. She'd said what she'd wanted to say, she'd made her offer and now it was up to him.

'But what would I do?' he asked blankly and that smile broke out again, impudent and teasing. Her toast and marmalade smile.

'You could sit on a throne and look regal.'

'I'd look pretty silly,' he told her and suddenly that tension zoomed back again. That link. She'd smiled, he'd smiled back and suddenly...

Wham. It was enough to knock the air right out of

him. He didn't have the faintest idea of why he felt like this, or even how he actually felt—all he knew was that he had to get to the other side of it fast. His world was being tilted and he'd spent his life desperately trying to keep his world right way up. After Lisle's death he'd sworn never to get that emotionally involved again—he'd never give anything or anyone the power to hurt him so much—but now…

Hell, what was he thinking? This was a marriage proposal she was making. Not a…

This was a marriage proposal!

He was just slightly out of his depth here. By about a mile.

'What would I do?' he asked again and if he sounded dumb that was because dumb was how he was feeling. Really, really dumb. What had she said? Knocked right over by a porrywiggle.

'For a start you'd fix your hospitals,' she told him, and lightness had suddenly faded. Her face was shadowed again. 'You know, we were here when Dominic got sick.'

'Here?'

'Warren and I were having a rocky patch,' she told him, and then gave a rueful smile. 'Actually our marriage was one long rocky patch. But my designs were getting known and I'd heard about the Alp'Azuri weavers and the yarns available here. I'd also heard the place was lovely. So Warren and I brought Dominic here for a holiday. But on the flight over I noticed Dom was bruising in a way we couldn't explain. By the time we'd been here for two days he was ill. And your hospitals… Have you spent any time at all in your hospitals?'

'No,' he said faintly. 'I've been back in the country for two weeks.'

'You've truly never been back since you left as a child?'

'My father wanted my sister dead,' he said, and after all this time it was still raw and painful to say it. 'And Jean-Paul never forgave my mother for taking Lisle and me to Paris. She tried desperately to explain. After my father died she tried to see him but he refused. And his hostility extended to me. So I figured it was a closed book. I haven't been back.'

'So it's your country—your responsibility—yet you don't know it.'

'That's right.'

She took a deep breath. 'OK. Then know this. Your hospitals are little better than third-world medical centres. They're a disgrace. You need to get in there and sort them out.'

He stared. 'You're very direct.'

'The word is bossy,' she said. 'But if I'm to make a supreme sacrifice…'

'A supreme sacrifice?'

Once again that cheeky grin. The grin that set him back. That made him feel…that made him feel like he didn't know how he felt.

'Marrying you,' she told him. 'Throwing myself away on a mere prince regent.'

Lightness. Maybe he should follow her lead. Maybe humour was the only way to cope with this. 'You figure you should hang out for the crown prince? For Edouard? For the real thing?'

'Maybe I should, but he might not want to marry me when he reaches maturity,' she conceded, smiling. 'My bloom of fabulous beauty may have faded a little by then. They tell me it happens. Bloom fading. It's caused by cabbage wilt or something.'

'Cabbage wilt?' He was so out of his depth that he thought he was drowning.

'It happens to all the best commoners. And sooner than you think,' she added darkly. 'So you'll be doing me a favour. You'll marry me and save me from the consequences of cabbage wilt.'

Deep breath. Levity wasn't going to work, he decided. She might be joking but he couldn't. She had to see how serious this was. 'Do you have any idea what you're suggesting?' he demanded.

'Sure I do. I'm suggesting marriage.'

Marriage. This was what his Uncle Lionel had suggested the day of Sarah's funeral, he thought, still stunned. 'Find someone else to marry—fast,' Lionel had said. But even Lionel had conceded the idea was fraught with peril. And now an unknown girl was calmly proposing.

Not an unknown girl. Jess.

'Only if you stay here,' she said and he met her gaze head-on. Their eyes locked and held. 'I'm only agreeing to marriage if you agree to stay.'

'You're really serious,' he said at last, and she nodded.

'I'm serious. I'm not the least bit interested in marrying anyone else—I've been there, done that, so I'm happy to stay married to you for as long as you need me to be. But your mother's not fit to be Edouard's guardian. Anyone can see that life's knocked her round. She'll make a lovely grandma but Edouard needs a parent. He needs you.'

He tried to make himself think. He tried to focus on Edouard. 'He loved you tonight…'

'And he'll love you. Don't stick him in a room with boa constrictors.'

'I'm expected back in Somalia.'

'That's nonsense,' she told him bluntly. 'I know enough about organisations such as Médecins Sans Frontières to know they'd say your first responsibility is to the people of your country.'

'This is not my country.'

'Oh, yes, it is,' she told him. 'You were born here. Your father was ruler. You're rich—'

'How do you know I'm rich?'

'I'm guessing that not even a creepy crown prince would keep his kids starving. I'm right, aren't I? You're rich.'

'Yes, but—'

'Look, stop running from it, Raoul. You're stuck between a rock and a hard place, so you might as well wriggle down and make yourself comfortable.'

'By marrying you.'

'It's a perfectly good offer.'

'So what would you get out of it?' he asked, and then watched as her face stilled and a wave of anger followed.

'I'd get a fairy-tale wedding, a prince, a tiara and I'd get to eat caviare and cream cakes for the rest of my life. Every girl's fantasy. What do you think?'

'I didn't mean—'

'Well, don't say it if you don't mean it,' she told him. 'You needn't worry. I don't want a thing except the reassurance that Edouard will be safe.'

'So why do you care?'

'For no reason,' she snapped, still angry. 'Except that no one else seems to have cared. Sure, you were doing your best in offering to marry Sarah, but if Edouard had been my nephew and he looked at me like he did tonight, I would have stuck my notice on the palace gate, married the first woman who offered and worried about the consequences later. I wouldn't have left him in the ghastly Cosette's care for one minute longer. If you knew how important a little boy's life is—'

'I do know.'

'Then do something,' she snapped. 'Marry me and take over your rightful role. You needn't worry that I'll take liberties. I'll do whatever you need to make Edouard safe and then you won't see me again. It's a very good offer, Raoul. Take it or leave it. But take it or leave it now.' She took a deep breath. 'Because, to be honest, I can't believe I'm doing this. I can't believe I'm saying it. But I am. Marry me, Raoul. Yes or no.'

He gazed into her face and she gazed back, her expression calm and determined. She was totally serious, he thought, and the realisation was astounding. She'd do this thing.

And in return… He'd have to stay here.

He could marry her and then leave after she'd gone back to Australia.

No. What was being offered was a gift, and the gift wasn't personal. It was a gift to Edouard and it was a gift to the people of Alp'Azuri. If he betrayed her trust, if he betrayed her promise…

He couldn't and she could tell that he couldn't. She was watching him, waiting for him to make a decision and there wasn't the least suspicion of mistrust on her face. She'd take his promise and she'd ask no questions.

He'd still be on his own—which was the way he'd planned his life. He simply needed to reorient his career. Incorporating Edouard.

Incorporating his country.

But not Jess. Jess only in name.

She was waiting on his decision and that decision had to be made now. He glanced through to the bedroom—and there was Edouard.

Edouard.

He'd been prepared to marry Sarah because of Edouard.

There was only one answer to be given.

'Thank you, Jess,' he told her. 'I would very much like to marry you.'

Raoul left soon after, walking away as a man stunned.

He might well be stunned, Jess thought as she prepared for bed. This marriage would affect her not at all. For Raoul, however, it would be life-changing. She'd thrown him a challenge he hadn't been able to refuse but she knew very well what it meant to him.

He'd decided to marry his cousin, Sarah, and then do what she intended—leave and return to his old life. But the marriage she offered came with strings—taking up his responsibilities—and she knew that he'd be feeling as if the floor had been swept from under him.

So she made no demur as he bade her a stunned goodnight and left her.

With Edouard.

Which had its own problems. She approached the bed and stared down at the child curled up in sleep. And her gut clenched in pain. To sleep with him…to feel the warmth of his little body…

No.

She'd sleep on the settee in the sitting room, she decided.

But when she was ready for bed she checked on Edouard again and found he was awake. His eyes were wide and scared, as if he'd woken midnightmare.

'Cosette,' he whispered, but it was a hopeless little whisper, as if he didn't really want Cosette, but she was all he knew—and who was this?—and no one would comfort him anyway.

Jess couldn't bear it. What was she about, thinking of her own pain when this little one was so needful? She sat down on the bed beside him and she took his hand.

'No, Edouard,' she said softly. 'Cosette's left me with you for a bit. You remember me. I'm Jessie. I'm the lady who gave you Sebastian.'

The terror receded from his eyes. Just a little. He'd remembered a small comfort. 'Sebastian,' he said and his spare hand searched the bedclothes and found the bear in question. But his fingers still clutched hers. 'Jessie,' he whispered and his eyes closed again.

She was held.

She should pull away.

But she didn't. She sat looking down at him. She moved slightly and his hand clutched her tighter. Finally she conceded defeat.

She was ready for bed. She didn't need to leave.

She slid under the sheets.

One warm little body sidled closer. Snuggled.

Oh, God.

What had she done? She lay and stared into the night, her emotions a kaleidoscope.

She'd agreed to marry Raoul.

More. She'd fallen for one little boy. She didn't want to do it—more than anything she was trying to hold herself rigid in the night—but he was so needful. It would have taken a superhuman effort not to put her arms around him and hold him close and let herself smell the clean-soap smell of a tiny child.

Dom…

She was going to choke. The emotions…

There was a faint knock on the door. She didn't answer. She couldn't. She was going to cry.

'Jess?'

It was Raoul. The door opened slowly and she could see his outline in the doorway. He was wearing a big, loose sweater instead of his dinner jacket. His body filled the doorway.

His presence filled the room.

'Are you OK?'

She couldn't answer. She was so close to tears. He approached the bed, and she looked up at him in much the same way Edouard had looked at her. Fearful. Not knowing what to say.

She saw his face twist and she knew that he realised what was happening.

'I wanted to walk,' he whispered, sitting down on the bed and laying his hand on her hair. It was a gesture she might have made to reassure Edouard. Like Edouard, she needed reassurance. She needed… Raoul?

'I had so much to think about,' he went on. 'I've spent half an hour wandering the gardens thinking of what I was going to do—how I was going to cope— and then suddenly I remembered that Edouard was still here. That I'd left Edouard in your room. And for you to sleep with Edouard…'

'It's OK,' she managed, and he shook his head. His fingers started raking her curls, almost absentmindedly.

'It's not OK,' he told her. 'Sure, I know it's something that you'll do and I can't think what else is to be done tonight, but I know what you're asking of yourself. After losing your Dominic, to hold Edouard… It's one of the bravest things I've seen and

I've been in some desperate situations in my time. Jess, how can I help? Shall I take him back to my room?'

She shook her head. Soundlessly. But she'd wept a little—just a little. He laid a finger on her cheek, he felt the damp track of tears and he swore.

'You're not responsible for Edouard,' he told her, almost fiercely. 'I'll not make you responsible as well.'

'It's OK,' she made herself say. 'He needs me. For tonight he won't let me go and I don't blame him.'

'But you've done enough.'

'I can't leave him.'

'Maybe not.' He sighed and glanced around, obviously working on a plan. 'Tell you what. You sleep with Edouard and I will, too.'

'What?'

'You needn't worry,' he told her and there was that crooked smile she was starting to know so well. 'I'm not insinuating myself into your bed. But you can't tell me that being here with him by yourself isn't painful.'

'Yes, but—'

'All I'm saying is that I'll be here, too,' he told her. He lifted a quilt that was lying over the foot of her bed and took a couple of pillows from the mound she'd discarded. 'I'll sleep on the settee,' he told her. 'Right here. It'll make it different. You're not sleeping alone with a child. You're sleeping with both of us. Sort of a pyjama party without the movies and the popcorn.' His fingers touched her hair again. Gently. Questioning. 'Will that help?'

How could it help? But strangely she knew that it would.

'There's no need,' she whispered and he nodded as if his question had been answered.

'There is a need.' He stooped, and ever so gently he kissed her. Lightly. Softly. Wonderingly. 'Sleep well, my Jess. My heroine. My bride. Sleep well and know that I won't burden you further.'

He left her then. She lay and listened as he made up the settee. It was crazy. There was no need. She couldn't sleep if he was here.

She heard him settle in his makeshift bed.

'Goodnight, Jess,' he told her.

She'd never sleep.

She lay with Edouard warm against her and Raoul not ten yards away.

'Just lie there and think of England,' Raoul's voice said into the night, and amazingly there was laughter behind the words. 'Or Australia. Whatever takes your fancy.'

She smiled.

She'd never sleep.

She slept.

CHAPTER SIX

THEIR marriage took place the next morning, before the rest of the world realised the inhabitants of the royal palace were even awake.

For that they had Henri to thank. The elderly butler did his rounds early—at six. He had found Cosette and the rest of the staff missing, and he discovered that Edouard was not in his bed. He'd then gone to find Raoul and found him missing, too. Finally, starting to panic but not panicked enough to tell Louise, he'd checked Jess's room, and his relief at finding them all present and correct was almost comical.

And when Raoul told him what he and Jess intended to do, he'd almost wept. He'd stood, stunned, while Raoul explained what was planned—and then he moved into action.

'Well, if you're going to marry I'd suggest you do it now,' he told them, smiling as if he'd been given the world. He glanced at the still sleeping Edouard. 'You leave the little one with me while you go and tie the knot,' he told them. 'I'll take him to his grandmother.'

'He might be upset,' Jess told him.

'He may well be,' Henri agreed. 'But what you're

doing is intended to make his life a whole lot less upset. It's the best idea I've heard of in my life. Get on, the pair of you. There's a magistrate down in Vesey. He's a friend of mine—not a government man—and he'll bend over backwards to make sure everything's done legally. Tie the knot before Marcel and his government cronies come up with objections, and be back here in time for breakfast. I'll have the champagne cold.'

He was brooking no argument. Even when Edouard stirred and woke he proceeded calmly, lifting the little boy—and attached teddy—into his arms before anyone could demur. Edouard whimpered a little, but Jess was there, pressing Sebastian close.

'You're going to your grandma now,' she told him. 'Henri will take you. Grandma wants to see Sebastian and his new trousers. Your uncle Raoul and I will be back soon.'

Edouard stared doubtfully from Raoul to Jess—but he was a child accustomed to whatever was thrust at him. His face shuttered a little but he sank against Henri's chest and allowed himself to be carried away.

His stoicism almost broke Jess's heart, but it firmed her in what she was doing. This marriage would give Edouard security and that was all that mattered.

'OK?' Raoul asked, as Henri disappeared with his charge. Jess nodded. She was feeling really strange, standing here with this man, in her nightdress and her bare feet—and she had a feeling this strangeness was just going to get a whole lot stranger. But she was right. This was a plan that could work.

'No doubt at all,' she told him. 'Let's get married.'

Raoul gave her a quizzical look and she managed to smile.

'There are not a lot of women who've said that to you, I bet,' she told him. 'Even among your thousand.'

He gave her a sideways grin at that. 'How do you know, Miss Cocky Boots?'

'Right.' She smiled, the strangeness easing in the face of his smile. 'I forgot. They're queued at the gate. All your brides. So let's give them the slip and get this bride safely hitched.'

He smiled back. That gut-twisting smile. The smile that changed things…

It couldn't be allowed to change things. This was a marriage of convenience, she told herself a trifle breathlessly as he disappeared to change and to shave. Her heart had no business twisting as it did at a stupid smile.

Even if that smile belonged to her bridegroom— and she was about to be married to one of the most gorgeous men in the world. And certainly the most eligible.

Forget about eligibility and gorgeousness, she told herself crossly. She had more important things to think about.

Like what to wear?

She really should have a little something in gossamer, she thought ruefully while she showered. A lavish something in white. And a diamond tiara or six.

Yeah, and a dozen bridesmaids and a glass carriage

and a team of silver horses and horse-guards and trumpets and…

And nothing. Ridiculous!

In the end she chose jeans and a windcheater. She wanted to attract as little attention as possible, she decided, and when she came downstairs to find Raoul she discovered he'd done exactly the same.

'Matching outfits,' he told her. 'The theme is denim.'

'Very nice,' she said and managed a shaky smile. 'We'll set a new trend. Is my limousine at the door?'

'How can you doubt it?' he demanded—and she went outdoors to find the battered gardener's van parked at the front steps.

'We're travelling incognito,' Raoul told her and she nodded. The gardener's van was fine by her. Limousines might have been the last straw.

She was feeling so strange here that if she woke and discovered this was all a dream she wouldn't have been the least surprised.

They were silent on the drive to Vesey. Down past the place where Sarah had crashed into her car. Down to the sleepy little city that was the capital of this country but in most countries would scarcely qualify as a city.

They found M. Marc Luiten at his breakfast. He was an elderly gentleman, long widowed, and as his housekeeper showed Raoul and Jess into his dining room he looked up from his omelette as if nothing in life had the power to surprise him.

'Ha. Raoul.' He waved a fork at the chairs on the other side of the dining table. 'Take a seat, Your Highness. Forgive me but you can't keep an omelette waiting.'

'Nor would we want you to,' Raoul said politely and he and Jess sat and drank the coffee the house-keeper produced and waited for the omelette to be demolished. It was. Then M. Luiten carefully mopped his moustache with his linen napkin and turned his attention to the pair before him.

'I know I should have called you Prince Raoul,' he growled, 'but I've known you since you were in short trousers. Too damned old for ceremony. Sorry about your brother. And your bride. Bad business.'

'That's what I'm here for,' Raoul told him directly. '*Monsieur*, this is Jessica Devlin. Jessie and I thought we might try again.'

The man stilled, his coffee-cup hanging midway from table to mouth. 'Say again?'

'We thought we might try to get me married before Marcel takes charge. If you're willing.'

M. Luiten turned his attention—carefully—from Raoul to Jess. He'd hardly noticed her before, she realised, and she wasn't surprised. Raoul's presence filled the room. He was a royal prince. She could well be considered a nobody.

The other half of a marriage of convenience?

'Who did you say this was?' the man said, and Jess smiled.

'Jessica Devlin.'

'The girl who smashed into Lady Sarah.'

She flushed but she didn't turn away. 'Yes.'

'Good job there,' the man said directly and turned again to Raoul. 'If you'd asked me, boy, I would have told you there was bad blood. I know Lionel advised it but your father's side of the family is nothing but trouble. Just look at Marcel.'

'Yes, but it left us in a mess,' Raoul said and the old man nodded.

'Don't I know it. Marcel and his cronies have been beside themselves with excitement. If they get their hands on the boy there'll be no stopping them.'

'If Jessica marries me then I'll stop them.'

Once again the old eyes perused Jessica. He surveyed her for a long moment and something lit behind his eyes. Hope?

'They say you're Australian.' The gruffness was suddenly gone, replaced by businesslike efficiency.

'I am.'

'Not married.'

'I have been.'

'Divorced? Widowed?'

'Divorced a year ago.'

'I don't suppose you have your divorce papers with you,' he said and there was a note in his voice that said this was important.

'I have, actually,' Jess told him. 'I carry a copy of them with my passport.' In the last few months of Dom's life she'd taken him on a frantic trip to the US to try a new treatment. Because of tight international child-custody laws, she'd had to carry all her papers with her. Divorce papers. Birth certificates. Statutory declarations from Warren that she had his permission to take Dom wherever she liked.

She had a document folder that she travelled with and she hadn't cleared it out. This morning she'd simply picked it up and shoved it into her jacket pocket.

The man took it, but he looked at her for a long, searching moment before he allowed himself to open the folder.

Then he adjusted his glasses low on his nose and read.

At the end, he laid the folder down and there was no mistaking the look in his eyes now. The flicker of hope had become a blaze of excitement.

'These are in order. Raoul…'

'I've never been married. You know that.'

'I know that. You brought your birth certificate?'

'Yes. Is there a time limit? Do we have to give notice?'

'No notice at all,' he said and his tone was expansive, joyful, exuberant. He rose and flicked back the curtains. 'It's a wonderful morning,' he told them. 'The garden's looking magnificent. What say I ask my housekeeper and my gardener to act as witnesses? I'll marry you right now.'

Thus they were married.

If they'd been a couple in love it would have been a marriage to remember, Jess thought as the strange little ceremony took place. M. Luiten spoke his own language but it was the hybrid of French and Italian

Jess knew well. And she'd made these vows once before.

'To have and to hold, for richer, for poorer, in sickness and in health, for as long as we both shall live.'

It might just work this time, she thought as Raoul made his own vows, strong and sure. He'd taken her hand and the warmth and the strength of him made this seem…right. Her marriage to Warren had been a crazy mistake and even at the ceremony she had been having doubts. But now…she would be this man's wife unto death.

Half a world away.

She looked down at the band of twisted gold Raoul was placing on her finger. That surprised her, but she liked it, she decided. Even though she'd be on the far side of the world, she liked it that she would be married to this man.

He was a husband to be proud of. A prince to be proud of?

'I now pronounce you man and wife,' M. Luiten said in a voice of supreme satisfaction. 'You may now kiss the bride.'

She pulled her hand away, jerking out of her reverie with a start. 'There's no need…'

But Raoul took hold of her hand again. He smiled, and it was different from any smile she'd seen before. This was full of satisfaction—and more. There was release in his expression. This was a happy ending, and both of them knew it.

A happy beginning for Edouard? A happy beginning for this tiny country?

Raoul wasn't the only one who was smiling. The housekeeper and the gardener were beaming their delight, and so was *Monsieur* Luiten. They were standing under a rose-arch surrounded by the spring borders of *monsieur*'s luxuriant flower garden. The first spring roses were unfurling above their heads. There were blue jays and there were bumble-bees…

The world was smiling.

'Jessie, you've given me a gift,' Raoul told her, and his smile was gentle. Reassuring. 'You've given this country—all of us—a gift. If any bride deserved to be kissed on her wedding day, it's you.'

'But—'

'No buts, Jessie. Hush and be kissed.'

His grip on her hands tightened. He stooped—and he kissed her.

And what a kiss. This was no feather kiss. This was no formal kiss of thanks. This was the kiss of a man claiming his bride. It was an absolutely spectacular kiss, planned and executed with precision and with style. Jess heard the collective intake of breath from housekeeper, gardener, magistrate…and then she heard nothing.

Her senses shut down right then.

Was it the day? Was it the simple words of the bridal vows that had affected her so much? Was it this glorious garden and the thought that she was married?

No. She knew it was none of these things. It was the man, pure and simple. It was Raoul's mouth claiming hers. It was his arms holding her close, tugging her into him, his strength, his warmth…

The taste of him. The smell…

Raoul.

She'd never felt like this. Never. It was as if some-thing had plugged in, turned on; some current that electrified a part of her she wasn't aware she pos-sessed. Raoul held her, kissed her and she opened her mouth to receive the kiss and wave after wave of pure, hot light flooded through her body. Changing her.

This wasn't right, she thought frantically. This wasn't how she was supposed to be feeling. This wasn't good.

Or was it?

No. Of course it wasn't. She was out of control. She hated being out of control. What was happening to her?

This wasn't her! But how he was making her feel… She wanted to sigh with pleasure, she thought, but how could she sigh? Maybe she could do without the sigh if she could take control of the situation, grab him and kiss him right back…

Did she really want to take control? Maybe she'd just submit.

How stupid could that be? How wrong?

It couldn't be wrong, she decided, or if it was it was too late to make such a call, because that was exactly what she was doing. She was submitting to a kiss that was driving her wild. It was transforming her from plain Jessie Devlin, Australian designer, Dom's mother, Warren's ex-wife, to someone she had no idea she could possibly be.

Princess Jessica?

Raoul's wife.

She liked it.

No. She loved it. She just…loved it.

The kiss went on and on, with neither party wanting to be the first to pull away. Why would she want such a thing? He was searching her mouth, plundering her lips with his tongue. His hands were pulling her closer, closer, while overhead the bumble-bees droned in the morning warmth, the flowers dripped their crimson petals and their audience beamed and beamed and beamed.

And when the kiss ended—as finally, inevitably, even a kiss such as this must end—they broke apart and Jess knew her life had changed. And more, she knew that it wasn't just she who was feeling like this.

Raoul's eyes were clouded, dazed, and he gazed into her eyes and she knew that he felt exactly the same as she did.

He wanted her. And she wanted him.

Well, why not? she demanded wildly of herself. She was no virgin bride and she knew how good it could be between man and woman. Even if that man had been Warren, it had once been fun. But Raoul… How much better with Raoul?

And Raoul himself…what had he said? He'd had a thousand women?

But this wasn't about wanting anyone, she told herself, striving desperately for logic. It was more. If she slept with this man, if she stayed with him much longer—then her heart would be given absolutely. She was so close to falling in love.

And love was stupid. Impossible. He was a royal prince and she was a convenient bride who'd now go back to the palace, twist off the wedding ring that he'd placed on her finger for show and forget about being a princess. She'd pack her bags and leave for Australia.

Leaving her husband behind.

He saw her confusion. How could he not? He put his finger under her chin and he lifted her face so he was looking straight down into her eyes.

'Don't look so bewildered, Jess,' he told her gently. 'It was just a kiss. No?'

'N…no.'

No? She was agreeing with him. Or disagreeing with him. She didn't know which.

It was just a kiss.

He'd had a thousand women.

He was a royal prince. Get a grip, Jess. She was looking dumb.

So explain it. Find some sort of reality.

'I'm sorry but I thought I'd better look moonstruck,' she managed. 'For our audience.'

She'd surprised him. She saw a flash of what could have been bewilderment in his eyes—but then the laughter returned and the mask was in place and he was turning his bride to face their audience.

To face the world.

'We've done it,' he said, smiling, and M. Luiten surged forward to kiss the bride, and so did the housekeeper and then so did the gardener, even though that ancient relic had hands that had just come out of the turnip patch and if Jess had been wearing white gossamer it would have been a disaster. But it was no disaster. She was a gardening type of bride. The bride wore denim...

'Now.' M. Luiten was rubbing his hands. 'I need to get everything here copied and sent to every dignitary in this country so there can be no possible doubt that this marriage is binding.' Then, as the housekeeper and gardener disappeared reluctantly back to their duties, he became even more direct. 'I've done my job,' he told them. 'Raoul, you take your bride home and consummate the marriage before anyone can possibly gainsay it.'

'No!' The two voices spoke as one and M. Luiten glanced from Raoul to Jess and back again.

'Is there a problem?'

'What are you talking about?' Raoul demanded. 'Consummate? How can anyone gainsay our marriage if it's not consummated?'

'It's in the ascendancy rulings,' *monsieur* told them—apologetically. 'It's to stop a child becoming Prince Regent and it dates from the times when princes were married off as children. The prince regent must be a partner in a consummated marriage.'

'No one told me that,' Jess said, weakly, and Raoul's hand gripped her shoulder in empathy.

'No one told me that either.'

'Welcome to reality,' M. Luiten told them. He looked doubtfully at the pair before him. 'But there's no problem, is there?'

'Please tell me we don't have to prove technically

that it's been consummated,' Jess managed, with visions of ancient traditions, groomsmen around the bed cheering the groom on, brides' mothers producing stained sheets… What was the modern equivalent? DNA testing? Surely not.

'No,' M. Luiten told them, but he cast an uneasy glance at the retreating back of his servants and waited until they were well out of earshot before he continued. 'But let's not take any chances. Just make sure you're nicely compromised, Jessie, my dear.'

Compromised. She thought back to all those historical novels she'd read—the ones *without* the groomsmen cheering. Compromising seemed to have been achieved quite easily when a girl's reputation was at stake. 'Raoul slept with me last night,' she ventured, and *Monsieur* Luiten beamed his approval.

'Very good. That will do it. Now you're married, do it again tonight.'

'Hey,' Raoul said, startled. 'We did *not* sleep together.'

'We did, too,' Jess said demurely, and nudged him meaningfully in the ribs. This type of consummation she could handle. 'Are you saying you didn't come to my chamber at midnight and stay until well after dawn?' She smiled at him—still demure. 'Dear?'

He choked. 'Yes, but…'

'There you go, then,' she said serenely. 'Consummated.' She turned back to M. Luiten. 'If there's any doubt then ask Henri. He burst in on us at dawn.'

'When you were compromised?'

'Well, sort of,' she said and Raoul choked again.

The magistrate gave him a doubtful glance. But he spoke to Jess. Of the pair, he'd obviously decided she was the sensible one. 'Someone well might ask Henri,' the old magistrate growled. 'There's a lot at stake here so make sure you get it right. Stay together tonight and make sure there are people about as witnesses.' And then his look of worry faded.

'I know you'll do the right thing,' he told them. 'You've done enough. The terms of the regency seem to have been fulfilled. Raoul, you're now the Regent. Ruling monarch for the next eighteen years until Edouard is of age. And your bride is the Princess Jessica.'

'Princess.' She wrinkled her nose. This was sounding more and more like some sort of crazy historical tale. How could this be happening? On this nicely normal morning, in this real-life setting? With this gorgeous prince beside her?

Forget the prince, she told herself desperately. Focus on yourself. Princess? It sounded ridiculous.

'I need to address you as Your Highness,' M. Luiten told her and she blushed from the toes up.

'I'm not—'

'Yes, you are,' he told her, very definitely. 'From this day forth. Now, off you go, the pair of you. Back to your castle. A prince and his princess forever. And me? I'll go back to a second cup of coffee—after I've attended to some photocopying and a few very important phone calls.'

'Not to the Press,' Raoul growled and Jess looked startled. The Press?

'No. Oh, no.'

'They need to know,' M. Luiten said, surprised. 'You can't keep this a secret. More, you don't want to. Marcel needs to be put in his place and the population needs to be told. Indeed, I can't think of any announcement that will be met with more joy in this country.'

'But…' Jess looked at Raoul for confirmation and he nodded. This, it seemed, was her call. 'I'm leaving the country as soon as I can,' she said. 'It would be so much better for everyone if the Press didn't learn of it until after I left.'

'So much better for everyone?' the magistrate prodded and she gave a shamefaced grin.

'Well…so much better for me.'

'A wedding without a bride.'

'That's what this is, after all,' she said. 'I'm a wife in name only. To pretend otherwise isn't going to work for a minute.' She blushed. 'OK, we'll get the consummation bit sorted but after that I'm out of here, and I'd like to be gone before there's any fuss.'

'Raoul?' The magistrate looked to Raoul for confirmation and he nodded.

'It's a big thing Jess has done for us,' he growled. 'We'll not ask more of her. Surely a wedding is enough.'

CHAPTER SEVEN

THEY drove away, stunned. Or Raoul was probably stunned, Jess thought. She definitely was.

Princess Jessica.

The name drifted in her head as they turned toward the town boundaries, and then started up the mountainside to where the fairy-tale castle nestled on an eyrie that looked out over all the land to the sea beyond. Over all this principality.

She was a princess. Going home to her castle.

She choked back laughter.

'What?' Raoul asked. He seemed to be deep in thought—or maybe he was just concentrating on the winding road.

'Do you think people will find out?'

'That we're married? Of a surety they'll find out. They must. Hopefully the fuss will wait until you're safely out of the country, but our marriage will have major consequences for everyone here.'

'I meant…back in Australia,' she said in a small voice. The enormity of what she'd done was just hitting home. She'd proposed to a prince and she'd married him. She thought back to her workrooms, where her staff were hopefully beavering away producing her latest designs. She might have a loyal staff but they weren't exactly deferential.

Princess Jessica. They'd think it was fantastic. Fantastic and very, very funny.

'My staff will give me heaps,' she said ruefully.

'Give you heaps?'

'They'll tease me into the middle of next week.'

'You can always sack them.'

'Oh, yeah, right. That's me. Princess Jessica sacking her staff because they're teasing her.' The feeling of unreality faded a little and she chuckled out loud. 'I'd like to see it. Besides, I've been transformed into a princess, not a wicked witch. You have your fairy tales mixed.'

'It seems so unreal?'

'It certainly does,' she told him. 'Bring on your magic wands. I can't believe this is happening. And tomorrow or the next day I have to get on the plane and go home, transforming back into being just me. A nine-to-five existence is going to seem crazy after this.'

He looked across at her curiously.

'You know, there's no need for you to continue with a nine-to-five existence,' he said gently. 'You'll never have to work again.'

That silenced her. She worked at it for a minute, considering his statement from all angles, but any way she looked at it it didn't make sense.

'Pardon?'

'As my wife, you'll receive a more than generous income from the royal exchequer.' He rounded a particularly tight bend and concentrated on straightening the car. 'You needn't worry about the morality of accepting it,' he told her. 'The people aren't taxed to pay your income. This royal family has wealth which goes back hundreds of years. You're very well provided for.'

Whoa. 'I'm not,' she said flatly. 'The idea's ridiculous.'

'You've done the country a service,' he said, just as flatly. 'You deserve to be compensated.'

'I told you,' she said, and she couldn't keep the surge of anger from her voice, 'I'm the owner of Waves. I'm very nicely off, thank you very much, and I have no intention of taking any of your money. Or any of your exchequer's money, whatever an exchequer is. People would say I married you for your wealth and there's no way I want part of that. And you can forget the princess thing. A princess can't be an Australian fashion designer. Princess Jessica sounds like some type of Kewpie doll, or a little girl's fashion label. How much respect would I get with a name like that?'

He smiled. 'A great deal of respect.'

'Not in the circles I move in.' She folded her arms and looked grumpily ahead. 'No way.'

'Jess,' he said, gently into the silence, 'you've pushed me to be Prince Raoul. Your conditions stipulate that I stay here—stay in the royal goldfish bowl. I can't escape royalty. You're either royal or you're not. We're both royal, from this day forth.'

'You didn't make any such stipulation,' she told him. 'And don't go doing the injustice thing to me. You were born a prince. I was born a nice little commoner and that's the way I intend to stay.'

'So you'll return to Australia with nothing.'

'With a certificate saying I have a very good-looking husband. With the satisfaction of having a really cute step-nephew who's being raised by people who love him. And,' she told him—giving him the most virtuous smirk she could manage, 'I have the truly noble gift of having saved a man by marriage. Saved a prince by marriage. How many girls can add that to their curriculum vitae?'

He chuckled. To her amazement he chuckled. It was the nicest sound, she decided. The best.

'OK,' he conceded, when laughter faded. 'It's a job well done. And it is a job well done, Jess.'

'Yep. So we'll get this consummation business over tonight and tomorrow I can leave,' she said promptly, and the smile which still lingered at the corners of his mouth disappeared. His brow furrowed. Royalty was displeased?

'Why so soon?'

'I need to be back.'

'You were here on a buying trip. You've done virtually no buying.'

She hesitated. Say it like it is, a little voice told her—so she did.

'It's not just wanting to avoid fuss,' she admitted. 'I don't want to get any more fond of Edouard.'

Or of his uncle, she added, but she didn't say that.

A thousand women? There was no way she intended becoming number one thousand and one.

'I'm not sure you can leave tomorrow,' he told her. 'There'll be formalities. I need to consult the lawyers.'

'Raoul, you can stay in my room tonight,' she said generously. 'Have as many people outside as you like so we prove the marriage is consummated. We'll stuff a tissue in the keyhole and you sleep on the settee. You can even stick an X-rated video on the telly if you like so our audience can have some sound effects. I'll close the bedroom door and won't listen.'

'Um…' he said faintly. 'Thank you.'

'Think nothing of it. That'll be the formalities over, but that's it. We're free to spend the rest of our wedded bliss safely on separate sides of the world.'

'Seriously, Jess…'

'Seriously,' she said. 'Seriously it's best this way. I leave here fast before there are any complications.'

'And you want nothing?'

'Nothing.'

'Jess, I can't let you…'

But she was no longer listening. She was staring ahead. There was a farmer walking steadily along on the verge. He was leading…

'Alpacas,' she breathed, suddenly totally distracted. 'Oh, Raoul, look at that.'

Three alpacas.

One large alpaca being led by a harness.

Two tiny alpacas, stumbling along behind.

'What the…?' He pulled the car to a halt, but she was out of the car before it had stopped.

Alpacas?

Raoul parked the van safely far off the road and emerged to find his bride crouched on the roadside. She was examining alpaca babies. Crias. One white. One brown.

Alpacas were the weirdest animals, he thought as he walked back along the verge. Crias—baby alpacas—were even more weird than their adult counterparts. They seemed a cross between a camel and a goat, and their faces looked as if they'd come straight off the pages of a comic book. They were quizzical, comical and very, very cute.

The sight of them brought back a rush of memories—of the time before his family had been ripped apart. Lisle had loved alpacas, he remembered. She'd had a pet one…

This day was turning into an emotional roller coaster. He took a grip—sort of—and attempted to move on.

'Jess, we can't stay here. It's not a safe place to park.'

'These are suri,' she told him, without looking up from admiring the babies. 'Do you know how rare these are?' She beamed up at the man leading the adult alpaca. 'You have twins. A boy and a girl. They *are* twins?' she asked him in his own language.

'Yes.' The man, an elderly farmer, dressed rough, seemed less than enchanted with his babies. 'Twins.'

She didn't notice his disenchantment. 'Twins are

about a one in fifty thousand chance in alpacas,' she told Raoul. 'What a blessing. And different colours…' She sat back on the grassy verge, smiling in delight. Their tiny faces peered back at her and she fondled each face in turn. 'What are you calling them?' she asked.

'A nuisance.' Like Raoul, the farmer didn't seem to want to stop. 'Miss…' He glanced up at Raoul, as if asking for help.

But then he froze. His face stilled in recognition.

'Your Highness.' His voice was a gasp and there was something else besides shock there. Fear? 'Prince Raoul?' he stammered.

It was definitely fear. This wasn't the first time he'd met fear when the locals recognised him, Raoul thought bitterly, momentarily diverted from Jess and her alpacas. His brother and his father had done some real damage. For this man to be afraid…

This had repercussions for the whole country. The population had been betrayed by their royal family and by their government. He closed his eyes as the realisation sank in one stage deeper. Jess was right in imposing her conditions. She might be able to walk away from this country, but he couldn't.

He was trapped.

He was also stuck at this roadside while his bride patted alpacas—and with the local farmer looking as if he was expecting to be shot for blocking the road.

He wasn't even blocking the road.

'Yes, I'm Prince Raoul,' he managed. 'Relax. I'm not about to bite.' He smiled down at the crias—even though the last thing he wanted to do was smile at alpaca babies. On top of everything else, there was a bit of domesticity happening here that he wasn't too sure about. Watching Jess cuddle babies of any sort... There was gut clenching going on inside him that he didn't want to think about.

'Where are you taking them?' he asked, trying to sound formal. Even prince-like. Royalty taking a benign interest in the peasantry.

He didn't get it right. The man looked astonished. Jess flashed him a glance that was almost amused and he thought: OK, maybe I don't have the royal thing down pat yet. There had to be a level between fear and bemusement. It needed work.

He could work on it better if Jess wasn't looking at him like...like...

'I'm taking them to the market,' the man said, but there was still caution behind his eyes as if he was afraid Raoul might turn on him at any moment.

'You're selling them?' Jess asked, diverted from Raoul. She looked up at the adult alpaca—who looked indifferently over her head out to sea—and then she looked at the babies again. 'You breed them?'

'Yes. I sell the fibre.'

'I know the suri fibre,' Jess said warmly. 'It's one of the reasons I came here. It's fabulous.' She frowned, fingering the babies' coats. 'These babies have the most beautiful fleece I've ever seen.' She twisted up to look at Raoul, explaining. 'Suri fleece is known throughout the world for its softness and its lustre. It just shines. And this is the best.' She went back to examining the babies, her frown deepening as she took in exactly what she was looking at. 'Surely these babies have the very best fleece,' she told the man. 'Why aren't you keeping them?'

'Ask Angel,' he said bitterly, and turned and spat over the cliff.

'Angel?'

'The mother.' The farmer poked the adult alpaca with a gentle nudge that spoke of exasperated affection. 'Angel had one baby and was only a little interested. Maybe I could have encouraged her to take it. But then she had the second and she turned away as if it was all too much trouble. I've tried and tried to get her to suckle but to no effect. And I've promised my wife that we can go down to Cieste to stay with our daughter, who's due to have a baby herself. Now we have these two to care for. Angel won't feed them. I won't be here to hand-raise them and I can't afford anyone to do it for me. So I'll sell them.'

'And what about Angel?' Jess sounded confused.

'I've brought her with me so the babies will walk behind,' the man said. 'I can't carry them down to the market and I can no longer afford to keep a truck. They follow Angel. But I won't sell Angel. She'll come home with me and we'll try again.' He brightened a little. 'She's young. Maybe another year's maturity will see her become a mother. And her fleece is wonderful.'

'So the babies will be sold alone.'

'Yes.'

'If you sell them…they'll be separated?'

'Probably,' the man told her.

'And to walk to market…' She stared down at the small animals in dismay. 'It's another two miles. They're too little to walk that far.'

Uh-oh.

Raoul could see where this conversation was going. Raoul saw Jess look from the tiny, wobbly crias to the van and thought: Yep, definitely uh-oh.

And then he cheered up. It was a very good thing he was driving the gardener's van rather than his really nice Lamborghini, he decided. He couldn't see alpacas in a Lamborghini—but he just bet that Jess could.

Sure enough, she was turning from the van to him, looking up at him with eyes that were damn near as cute as the alpaca babies'. Maybe even cuter?

'We can take them with us, can't we, Raoul?'

'They won't all fit,' Raoul told her. No way. Angel was taller than he was, and how did you get a dopey alpaca to duck its head? 'We won't get *monsieur* and his three alpacas in the van at once.'

'But we need only take the twins.'

'And come back for *monsieur*?' If he sounded confused it was because he *was* confused.

'No,' she told him. 'There's no need.' She turned back to the farmer. '*Monsieur*, if I buy your babies you won't need to go to market.'

Silence.

'You're going to buy the alpaca babies?' Raoul said cautiously.

'Yes.'

'Um…Jess, you're going back to Australia.'

'Yes, but these are the perfect gift for Edouard,' she told him, obviously exasperated at his lack of instant comprehension. 'Edouard doesn't need a nursery full of stuffed boa constrictors. He needs friends. Alpacas are the nicest friends a little boy could have. If he bottle-feeds these two and you help him care for them, they'll be his friends for life. And I'll buy the fleece from him every year. It's just the most wonderful solution for everyone.'

Yeah. Right.

There was only one problem. What had she said?

If you help him care for them...

'We don't want alpacas,' Raoul said bluntly, and she eyed him in astonishment.

'Why ever not?'

Why not? Hell, think of something. There were emotional chasms yawning all over the place.

'Where would we keep them?' OK, so it wasn't a great try but it was the best he could do.

It didn't cut the ice with Jess. She grinned. 'Oh, now you're being ridiculous. You're living in that grand palace. You have stables, and pastures and servants...'

'We don't have servants.'

'For now because of that horrid man's threats. But you will as soon as it's known we're married,' she told him in English, beginning to sound exasperated. 'Raoul, what are you saying? That Edouard can't have these babies? You know how much he needs them.'

No, but I don't, Raoul thought as he stared down

at the roadside and watched this woman who was now his wife stroking the baby alpacas. Or I don't want...

He didn't know what he didn't want.

Somalia was much less complicated than this, he decided. His head was starting to spin. Give him medicine and life-and-death drama any day.

The farmer had been watching the pair of them in increasing bemusement. The fear he'd shown as he'd first discovered Raoul's identity had faded. He was obviously confused—but there was one important fact starting to emerge that he didn't intend to lose sight of.

'The lady wants to buy my twins?' he asked, and Jess moved into action.

'The lady definitely wants to buy your twins,' she told him 'How much?'

'These are very rare. Very rare twins.'

'Yes. How much?'

The man paused. He looked at Raoul to Jess and back again.

And he named a sum that made Raoul blink.

It didn't make Jess blink. 'I'll pay it,' Jess said, and she beamed and opened her handbag. 'Oh, and I'll give you my cell-phone number in case Angel changes her mind. I've heard of alpacas who finally decide they're mothers after they've been separated. If that happens I don't mind bringing them back and seeing if we can reunite them.'

'Hey, wait a minute.' Raoul thought about it and frowned. First there was the cost. Then there were other considerations. Lots of considerations.

He'd focus on the cost first. 'Surely a couple of straggly little alpacas on bandy legs can't be worth this much?' he asked and got a derisive look from his new wife for his pains.

'I'm not asking you to pay for them,' she told him. 'Though ten minutes ago you were telling me I could have an income for life. Just as well I didn't take you up on it, eh? I might have discovered your ideas of income and mine are miles apart.' She flicked through the contents of her bag and produced a cheque-book and pen. 'And don't cast aspersions on my babies,' she told him as she wrote. 'Bandy legs? Hmmph.' She smiled back at the farmer. 'Who do I make this out to?'

The farmer told her. His impatience was gone and he was beaming as happily as Jess was.

The only one not deeply satisfied with this arrangement was Raoul.

'Australian cheques won't work here,' he said weakly—for want of anything else to say—and Jess gave him a look of pure pity.

'I'm here on a buying expedition. If you think I'd come on a buying trip without local currency you're not thinking straight.' She smiled up at the farmer. 'I'm sorry about my husband,' she told him. 'He's being obtuse.'

'Your…husband?' the man said. He took the cheque Jess was proffering and he gazed at it in astonishment. But his face cleared as he read her name. 'No. This is not the royal name,' he said. He glanced across to Raoul, man to man, dealing with the vagaries of womenfolk. 'She's made a mistake, no?'

'About the alpacas?' Raoul told him. 'Yes. She definitely has made a mistake.'

'I have not made a mistake about the alpacas,' Jess said, indignant, but the man wasn't listening.

'About you being her husband?'

'I…no.' Hell, what else was he to say?

'You're married?' The farmer's face was a montage of emotion, changing minute by minute. 'This woman is your wife?'

'Yes, but…'

'But your fiancée died.' The farmer's thoughts were obviously racing as he tried to work things out. 'All was lost. This is the Australian woman who was in the accident, no?'

'Yes.'

'And this woman says you are her husband?'

'Yes.'

'Then you're married to this woman?' he said, insisting on getting this point clear.

Jess was no longer listening. She'd moved on. She was lifting the littlest alpaca across into the van. Put it in the back, Raoul thought, but no, of course she wouldn't do anything so logical. She was opening the passenger door and popping it onto her seat.

'Yes,' said Raoul, distracted. 'For my sins, I've married her. Jess, for God's sake, don't put them on the upholstery.'

'I'll cuddle them,' she said. 'They're too little to

stay in the back. They'll slide everywhere and they'll fall over. Look at their wobbly legs.'

'I bet they're not housetrained.'

She grinned. 'Just lucky the van isn't a house, then.' She returned and stooped to lift up the next cria. 'What am I going to call you?' she demanded of the second baby—a tiny chocolate alpaca with a face like Mickey Rooney's.

'Balthazar,' Raoul said weakly—and he knew he was lost right then.

'Balthazar.' She paused and gazed up at him in astonishment. 'Why Balthazar?'

'After…after an alpaca I once knew.' An alpaca who looked like Mickey Rooney.

'You've known an alpaca?'

'Lisle…'

Her face changed, just like that. Crumpled. Her eyes creased into distress. 'Lisle. Oh, Raoul, of course. What have I done? If you really don't want them…'

She understood. He stared down at her as she knelt, gathering the second cria into her arms and looking up at him in distress, and he thought, She understands.

He didn't do emotion. He didn't need this empathy bit. And he didn't want her to look at him like this.

The last thing he wanted from this woman was sympathy. It did something to him, something he wasn't sure he could handle.

Or maybe he was sure he couldn't handle it.

'I'll buy them now, but I'll find someone else who can keep them,' she was saying, immeasurably distressed. 'If they're going to cause you sadness then of course you won't want them up at the castle. There are weavers down in the valley who'd love to take these on. I can pay for their keep. I won't—'

'Just put them in the van, Jess,' he said, trying for dryness, but her look of distress intensified.

'Look, if you don't want to do even that much I'll understand. I can call a taxi.'

'A taxi? Here? And for non-housetrained alpacas?'

'I'll pay more for cleaning.' She jutted her chin. 'Raoul, I don't want to hurt you.'

And there it was. A declaration, just like that. *Raoul, I don't want to hurt you.*

What was she doing right now, by looking at him like this?

Get a grip.

'Look, this is dumb,' he told her. 'Of course we can keep them. And you're right. Edouard will love them.'

'But if they remind you of Lisle…'

'Maybe I need to be reminded of Lisle.' He caught himself, tried to rethink—but he knew that he was right. 'Maybe Lisle would tell me to get over it.'

She looked up at him, uncertain. 'Lisle would want you to take these home?'

'I guess she would.' He managed a smile, albeit a lopsided one. 'OK, I know she would. Even if I was driving the Lamborghini.'

That diverted her. 'You drive a Lamborghini?'

'Not when I'm transporting alpacas.'

She stared, seemingly dumbfounded. 'My husband drives a Lamborghini,' she said at last, and her look of sympathy was replaced by awe. And, amazingly, laughter. It was always there, Raoul thought, dazed. Ready to flash out at any opportunity. Life had kicked her round but still she laughed. 'Ooh, I so want Cordelia to know this.' She chuckled, including them all in her laughter. 'Cordelia is my cousin,' she told the farmer. 'She thinks she's the ant's pants because her husband drives a Porsche.'

'Ant's pants?' said the farmer. He sounded as dazed as Raoul was.

'Jess,' Raoul managed, trying desperately to get back on track. The world seemed to be spinning and he felt dangerously close to falling off. 'Leave the explanations. Just get the babies into the van.'

'She *is* your wife,' the farmer said, abandoning distractions and getting back to basics as well. To what was important.

They should have swapped to speaking English, Raoul thought ruefully. But Jess was fluent; they'd been speaking to the farmer in his own language and it would have seemed rude to swap. But now...he'd heard every word. Including ant's pants. And including the rest.

'I remember the Princess Lisle,' the farmer said, softly as if he was remembering something that gave him pleasure. 'You know...' he looked at Raoul, obviously trying to see in him the child that he'd once been '...you and your sister were born two days after my own daughter was born. My wife was so upset when they said the little girl—your sister—had problems. And then the old prince sent you away.'

'We need to get on,' Raoul said, more roughly than he intended, and the man beamed.

'Of course you do. You're taking the crias to the little prince?'

'He needs them,' Jess told the farmer and he nodded.

'We were so afraid... We have all been so devastated that the Comte Marcel would get his hands on the little prince.' He turned to Raoul, and his face revealed a mix of emotions that were clearly threatening to overwhelm him.

'You married this woman so that Comte Marcel wouldn't control the prince. So his grandmother could love him.'

There was only one answer to that. When the man looked at him like that...when he was feeling as he was feeling...

'Yes,' he said and the man blinked. He stood and stared at them for a long moment, and then he stared down at Jess.

Then he lifted the cheque and ripped it in two.

'I'm not a wealthy man,' he told them. 'But you give me hope. How does that compare to the value of a cheque?'

'Hey.' Jess rose, still hugging her baby. *'Monsieur,* I wanted you to have that money,' she told him. 'Prince Raoul has enough. He even drives a Lamborghini.'

'This money was yours.'

'Now I feel like a rat,' Raoul told them.

'Good,' Jess said. *'Monsieur—'*

'I will not accept payment from you,' the man said. 'Not in a million years. Take these babies to the little prince, and God bless.'

'Well, thank you,' Jess said, clearly disconcerted. 'You're very good.'

'It's you who is good.' He smiled. 'I'll take Angel home and maybe she will miss her babies and repent and maybe she won't but even if she won't I know they've gone to a noble cause.'

'They'll piddle on the van seats,' Raoul said darkly but they were all smiling.

There was nothing left to do.

Jess loaded the second baby. She sat, overwhelmed by alpacas, smiling supremely, and once more Raoul steered the van toward the castle.

And on the road behind them the farmer smiled and smiled.

'I have been very generous, no?' he demanded of Angel, who was yet to notice that her babies had disappeared. 'I have been wonderful. As this marriage is wonderful. But then, if this marriage is wonderful, why doesn't the entire world know? And who is to tell them but me?' He grinned. 'I have been very wonderful but the fees for news stories are very, very excellent. I have, my Angel, what the world calls a scoop. Let's see how fast we can walk to the nearest farmhouse. I need to make a very important phone call.'

CHAPTER EIGHT

IT TOOK twenty minutes to get from where they'd met the farmer to the palace gates.

In that twenty minutes the world had woken up.

One phone call from the farmer had produced immediate results. There had been huge media interest in the death of Lady Sarah. Everyone in the country knew the terms of the royal succession, and apart from Marcel and the politicians who would benefit, everyone had been devastated. There was general consensus that the little prince should stay with his grandmother and there had been hope that Raoul would prove a better ruler than his predecessors. Sarah's death had dashed those hopes, but there was still avid interest in this Prince Raoul who the country knew so little of and who had lost so badly.

So there'd been media camped up at the palace gates, waiting to get interviews, photos, anything. That interest had died back over the past few days, so much so that they'd been able to get out this morning simply by driving the gardener's van. No one had been stirring in the camp. No one had expected anything except maybe a statement of misery as the royals moved out.

But the farmer's phone call had changed things.

As they approached the castle gates, the media seemed to burst from nowhere. Photographers and reporters and their associated equipment were spread over the road and their excitement was obvious from five hundred yards.

'Uh-oh,' Raoul muttered.

'M. Luiten must have told them,' Jess whispered, horrified.

'Maybe it was your own declaration down the mountain,' Raoul said drily. 'You can hardly go round calling me your husband if you don't want anyone to know.'

'But the farmer didn't have a phone.'

'Maybe not but I'm guessing he and Angel found a phone faster than I can drive.'

'So you're saying this is my fault?'

'Absolutely.' He grinned.

'Raoul…'

'It'll be fine,' he told her. 'Pretend you don't speak our language.'

'I can do that. And they can hardly photograph me,' she said, cheering up as she hugged her babies. Raoul was smiling his reassurance. It couldn't be all bad. 'I'm covered in alpaca.' She peered out at the pack ahead, blocking the road. 'Can they stop us? Can't we keep driving?'

'Squashing the odd reporter?'

'I think reporters are unsquashable,' she said doubtfully. 'It's in their job description.'

'A bulldozer probably wouldn't squash this lot and

we're going to have to face this some time,' he told her, drawing reluctantly to a halt. 'We might as well face this now.'

'Wrong.'

'Wrong?'

'You're going to have to face this some time,' she told him. 'I'm going back to Australia.'

'After the Press conference, my love,' he told her. 'Which is scheduled to start right now.'

My love...

Why had he called her that? Jess sat in the passenger seat and hugged Balthazar and Whatshername while Raoul got out of the van and started answering questions.

He'd called her my love. It had been a throw-away line, she thought. A dry reference to that fact that they were now married. It didn't mean anything.

Heck, why was she thinking about two little words when she had so much more to think about? She shoved the two words away—not so far that she couldn't haul them up at some later date and inspect them, but far enough away so she could think about what was happening.

The window on her side was closed but Raoul had left his side open and she could hear every word. There were microphones in his face and cameras flashing. Ugh. She slunk down and held her alpacas close; forming a barrier from the crowd trying to peer in.

The babies wriggled, not liking the flashes.

'Shush,' she told them. 'We're not on display here. Raoul is.'

Her husband?

He'd called her his love. Damn, the words wouldn't stay where she'd put them. They were demanding immediate inspection.

'I bet that's what he called every one of his thousand previous women,' she told the alpacas, and then she corrected herself. 'I mean…they're not previous to me. I do not make one thousand and one.'

She wasn't making sense, even to herself.

She might as well listen to what was going on outside.

'We've received reports that you're married.' That statement in many different forms was being thrown at him from all sides.

Did he mind? He seemed assured, Jess thought. A prince in charge of his world. Or maybe as a doctor working where he'd been, he'd had practice handling the Press. Whatever, Raoul had himself settled now. He was leaning back against his closed car door, protecting his bride as he faced the media.

'That's right,' he told them. 'I'm married. As of an hour ago.'

There was a moment's shocked silence—a vast aura of stunned amazement from a contingent of the media who clearly were unused to being this shocked—and then a surge of questions.

'When?'

'Why?'

'Who?'

'Is it the lady in the car?' someone demanded, and Raoul's quiet yes led to another moment's silence.

Jess pushed the lock down on her side of the van. Just in time. Someone grabbed her door and tried to open it.

She manoeuvred Balthazar so he was between her and the window.

'Questions to me, please,' Raoul told them. 'My wife is understandably overwrought.'

Overwrought? She thought about that, while she cowered behind her alpacas. Overwrought. It made her sound like a frail little princess.

Balthazar licked her hand and she thought, No, I'm not frail. She hugged the little cria closer. It was she who should be reassuring Balthazar. What was he doing licking her?

'This is a marriage of convenience, right?' someone else asked and Raoul let the question hang, as though considering. But obviously he'd decided that the only way forward here was with honesty.

'You all understand the rules of the succession,' he told them. 'And I'd imagine you all understand what's happened. My mother desperately wants to be permitted to raise her grandson. The Comte Marcel refuses her that right. My cousin, Lady Sarah, agreed to marry me so that the succession could stay with me. Tragically, Lady Sarah's untimely death meant that my nephew would be placed in the viscount's care on Monday. Ms Devlin kindly made the offer of marriage and I was left with no choice but to accept.'

Hey! She thought about that. It sounded really reasonable, she decided, but there were parts of it that she couldn't quite like. *I was left with no choice but to accept…*

Poor Raoul, forced into marriage with the likes of her.

Hmmph.

Listen some more, she told herself. Let's not get your knickers in a knot quite yet. Focus.

'Has Ms Devlin been married before?'

'Yes. As had Lady Sarah. That's no impediment to the succession.'

'Will you stay in the country now?'

A moment's hesitation. Then, 'Yes. There is a lot that needs attending to in this country. I'm prepared to stay here and see that changes are made.'

There was a general rumbling of interest, and Jess heard the transparent murmur of approval. And… hope?

But they were focusing back on her again.

'Will Ms Devlin help care for the prince?'

'Ms Devlin intends to leave for Australia tomorrow and have nothing further to do with us.'

'She's now a princess, right?' someone asked.

'Legally, yes.'

'We need photographs.'

'I'm sure you'll understand that my wife was in a severe car accident only a week ago,' he said, smoothly. 'She's not up to photographs or answering questions.'

Ooh, she was a real wilting violet. Jess could feel herself getting frailer by the minute.

'If she's not up to answering questions, how can she be up to deciding to marry you?' someone demanded. 'Surely that's a bigger question than any we can put to her?'

The train of thought took hold. There were more flashes in her direction. Wall of alpaca, with bride somewhere behind.

'Was this really her idea or yours?' someone else asked. 'She's been injured and stuck in the palace until now. Has anyone seen her apart from palace insiders?'

'She's not a bride by coercion, is she?' someone else called. 'It doesn't look good.'

Raoul was starting to sound exasperated. 'If you knew Jessica you'd never suggest such a thing. Coercion!'

Coercion, Jess thought blankly. Poor little injured traveller, tied with silk cords, or maybe chained in a dripping dungeon, rats running over her feet, surrounded by a few skeletons for good measure, whipped, starved, until finally she agreed to marry the wicked prince.

She grinned.

But maybe it wasn't funny. The questions were getting nastier.

'We can suggest what we like,' someone else said. 'We're damned sure Marcel will be suggesting there's been a measure of intimidation. Or bribery. He's going to have kittens when he finds out you're married. And married to an accident victim who's not even well enough to answer questions...'

Enough.

Princess Jessica flicked up the lock on her door. She placed the little white alpaca, as yet unnamed, across onto Raoul's seat and attempted to do the same with Balthazar. But Balthazar had decided that the only thing standing between him and the mortal terror of the flashes was Jess. He gave a tiny flickering whimper and stuck his nose into her armpit. When she tried to haul him out he whimpered again.

She sighed.

'OK, let's do this together,' she told him. 'Princess in chains and alpaca in armpit. A lethal combination, I don't think.'

But it had to be done. She hugged Balthazar close, and she emerged to face the music.

The media moved, just like that. Bride emerges from car...

For a moment Jess couldn't speak. There was no chance to speak. The moment her door opened the cameras spun to face her, and flashlights went crazy.

Balthazar nuzzled closer and she knew how he felt. Give her an armpit to hide in and she'd be right in there! But Raoul—her only available armpit—was on the other side of the van and she'd emerged to defend him.

Right. Let's do it.

'You're scaring my babies,' she said, clearly and loudly, and everyone took a step back.

'You speak our language,' someone said, and she gave him a look of astonishment.

'Why wouldn't I?'

'But you're Australian.'

'The two things are not necessarily incompatible.'

'Jess, hop back into the van,' Raoul said uneasily. He turned to the Press, appealing to their better nature. 'Jess isn't well. I'll drive her into the palace grounds and come out and speak to you for longer.'

'I'm sorry to have to contradict you, my love,' Jess said, giving him her most domestic smile, 'but I'm very well. Far too well for these ladies and gentlemen to imply you've coerced me into marriage while I was ill.'

There was another murmur of surprised delight. The attention, if anything, intensified.

'You called His Highness "my love".'

'So I did,' she agreed cordially. 'What do you call your wife?'

General laughter.

'Does he call you "my love"?'

'He started it.' She looked across the van roof to Raoul, she lifted her brows in mock-enquiry and she smiled. 'Didn't you...dear?'

'Um...' He appeared gobsmacked. Maybe he was gobsmacked.

'Why did you agree to marry His Highness?' someone asked and Jess allowed her domestic smile to become a trifle complacent.

The reporter who'd asked the question was younger than Jess. Jess smiled at her, woman to woman. 'His Royal Highness was desperately in need of a bride,' she said virtuously. 'And I was available. I've done a very good deed.' She grinned across at Raoul. 'I know, Prince Raoul has major problems in terms of eligibility. He's thirty-five, he's desperately good-looking, he's kind to his mum, he loves his nephew, he's a doctor—and I imagine he looks really gorgeous in a white coat. Oh, and did I mention that he's rich?' She let her smile become prim. 'But I've put all that aside. I thought, no, I can take pity on him and marry him. Charity is my middle name.'

There was general laughter—delighted laughter—and the attitude of the entire Press corps changed. She had them on her side, just like that.

'So now you're Princess Jessica,' the reporter said and Jess raised amused eyebrows.

'I guess I am. As long as no one expects me to wear a tiara.'

'What did you wear at your wedding?'

'What I have on.' She glanced down at her jeans, which were now liberally adorned with alpaca hair and the odd bit of mud from tiny hooves.

'With or without the alpaca?' someone demanded.

'Hey, I had to have bridal attendants,' she told them and everyone laughed again. She flicked a glance down into the van, just to make sure her Baby No. 2 was OK—and winced. 'Um, Raoul...'

'Yes, dear?' He seemed stunned.

'Um...what you were most afraid of...in the van...'

Distracted, he stared into the van window. And saw what she was seeing.

'Oh, God...'

The media were now totally on their side. From being aggressively curious, they were suddenly a group of people enjoying themselves. Raoul hauled the door of the van open and gingerly pulled out the cria—holding her at arm's length. He handed her to the nearest reporter.

'Hey, I don't want it,' the man said and Raoul grinned.

'This is my first royal command,' he told him. 'Take her away.' His grin deepened. 'Consider it a scoop.'

More laughter and the reporter carried her gingerly to the road verge. Just a bit too late.

Actually, quite a lot too late.

'You're going to explain the condition of his van to Georgio,' Raoul told Jessica wrathfully—and she giggled.

'Yes, dear.'

They were entranced. These reporters must have been bored stupid for the last few days. Maybe they'd been bored stupid for years, with a not very savoury royal family to report on. Now... Jess could see headlines forming in their eyes, but she could also see real pleasure.

'You're not really leaving us tomorrow?' someone asked and the laughter died.

She swallowed.

'Yes, I am.' There was nothing else to say. She thought briefly, maybe she could stay and keep on with her buying expedition, but she knew now that such a thing would be impossible. She'd have reporters trailing her every inch of the way, and Raoul would be left...

She glanced across at Raoul and thought, no, she had to get away. From Raoul?

'I don't live here,' she said gently. 'I've made this marriage so that Prince Edouard can be safe, and so Prince Raoul can set in train the reforms he badly wants to make. But I've done that by agreeing to the marriage itself. There's no reason for me to stay longer.'

'What about all those things you just listed regarding His Highness's eligibility?' the woman reporter demanded, and Jess met her look head-on and thought: Uh-oh.

Woman to woman.

She looked away but...was she that transparent?

She couldn't be transparent.

'Hey, I've saved the world,' she said, trying for laughter again. 'I'm like Superman turning back into nobody, popping my cape back in the cupboard until the next crisis. My job here is done. Back to the real world.'

Laughter. But still the question. 'But you'll stay married to His Highness forever?'

'If that's what it takes,' she told them, and her chin jutted again, definite on this point at least. 'I'll not marry anyone else.'

'Because of the gorgeous white coat?' the woman reporter teased and there was more laughter.

'I haven't actually seen the white coat,' she admitted. 'And maybe it's just as well if I don't. As I said, my job here is done. I'm leaving tomorrow.'

'Let us photograph you together,' someone begged

and she hesitated but then she glanced across at Raoul and his eyes were sending her a message.

Let's do this. Let's get it over with.

So she nodded. She walked across to the verge where Whatshername was starting to fret again. She handed Balthazar to Raoul and she lifted Whatshername into her arms. Then she turned and smiled at the media. With her husband. And her children?

'OK,' she told them. 'Take as many pictures as you like. Behold the royal family.'

Raoul was smiling, relaxing, seemingly enormously relieved. He moved in close and he held her around the waist with the arm that wasn't holding Balthazar.

A smiling couple holding an alpaca apiece.

Raoul was holding her. She was pulled tight against him as the photographers took aim. She felt…she felt…

She didn't know how she felt. Very, very confused?

I definitely do not want to see that white coat, Jess thought grimly as she pasted on her very nicest camera-facing smile. If one arm could do so much damage, imagine what a white coat could do. There was such warmth, such strength…

His smile…

I do not want to see that white coat, she told herself again. I mustn't see it. I need to get out of here fast!

'You were incredible.'

Somehow they'd got away. Once they were inside the palace grounds the gates swung closed behind them. Without servants the castle forecourt was deserted. They emerged to soft sunshine and silence—and strangeness. Married life?

'I can't believe how you twisted them around your little finger,' Raoul was saying. He lifted Whatshername out of the van and set her on the lawn.

'Sheer idiocy,' Jess told him, taking Balthazar to join his twin.

'There was no idiocy about what you just did. You've saved our bacon. You have the Press on our side. There'll be no questions about our marriage. Marcel won't have a leg to stand on if he tries to drum up support to kick us out.'

'Will he do that?'

'He was certainly making noises before I married Sarah. But tomorrow the country will wake to you and your alpaca twins and the knowledge that I'm taking over. I already explained my logic to the Press before Sarah died. The population knows my marriage will mean free elections and a move to a proper democracy.'

'Where will that leave you?' she asked curiously and he shrugged.

'As Regent I'll get to sign all important papers. I can dissolve parliament if I wish—as I'll do now—but there's no way I'll do that after we get a decent government. I'll even be moving to change the constitution so that no ruling prince ever has the powers that I have again. It's time this country moved out of the Dark Ages.'

'You have all these powers?' she asked cautiously. 'Even if you're just Regent?'

'Hey, there's no just about it.' He was watching the two little alpacas nose each other in the morning sun, then settle down on the lush lawn for a nap. 'For the next eighteen years I'm effective ruler.'

'The same as a king.'

'If you like.'

'But with a retirement date.'

'Mm.' He grimaced. 'It'll be the only thing that keeps me sane. I get to retire at fifty-three.'

'And go back to Somalia?'

'Maybe.'

'You know,' she said cautiously, 'what you've just done…I hadn't really thought it through from your angle. I've been married. I've had a son. But you… If you're settling here for eighteen years, won't you want a wife?'

'I already have one.'

'No, but a real one.'

'You're real enough for me, Jess.'

She gave him a distracted smile. 'You know what I mean,' she told him. 'Not one in name only. You might find it hard to move on to your next thousand women in the confines of the royal spotlight.'

'My next thousand women?'

'You said you'd had a thousand,' she told him. They were watching the babies still nuzzling each other in sleepy satisfaction as they wriggled down on the grass.

'Right,' he said faintly. 'I'd forgotten.'

'So if you want a divorce…' she said.

'I don't want a divorce.' He hesitated. 'I don't think I can get a divorce. Not until I'm fifty-three.'

'We might be able to manage one while Marcel's not looking,' she said. 'If you meet someone highly desirable we could fix it so we were divorced and you were remarried two minutes afterwards so Edouard will still be safe.'

'I don't want to be divorced.'

It was a strange statement. A weird statement. It hung between them, a bit like an upraised sword. Threatening damage?

Surely threatening peace.

'You never know,' she managed and if she didn't manage to get her voice to work quite right then who could blame her? By anyone's reckoning it had been a very strange morning.

'These babies need feeding,' Raoul told her and his voice was suddenly rough. She looked at him strangely. Was he feeling like she was?

Alpacas. Think of alpacas. What had he said? The babies need feeding?

'Um…sure.'

'Do you have any idea what to feed alpaca babies?'

'Alpaca milk, preferably,' she said. 'But failing that, my best guess is skimmed milk. We can ring a vet and find out. But I'm sure skimmed milk won't hurt in the interim.' She thought about it. 'We need baby bottles. Do you suppose there's somewhere in the kitchen who can find such things?'

'I doubt it.'

Goodness, was there no end to what she had to do for this family? She was going to turn out bossy, she thought, and then she thought of Cordelia and grinned.

Cordelia would tell her she'd been born bossy.

'You take the babies across to the stables,' she told him. 'I'll go see what I can find.' She hesitated, seeing her own doubt reflected in his eyes. 'You know, weird as it seems, rooting around in a castle kitchen to see if I can find baby bottles is strangely appealing.'

'No stopping for toast and marmalade,' he told her and her smile faltered a little. Damn, how was it that he made her feel like this? As if he knew her so well? As if there was a part of her that was missing? Or had been missing up until now.

'I'm off on a bottle hunt,' she told him, more tersely than she'd meant. 'You go find our babies a bed.'

'Right,' he told her and there was still that strange look on his face. 'Right.'

It took her longer than she'd intended. Henri and Louise and Edouard were nowhere to be seen, and there were certainly no servants to ask, so she had to search the kitchen herself. She found what she was looking for—in the end she found a whole cupboard filled with baby paraphernalia—but then she had to figure out how to operate the microwave. She failed dismally. Finally she found a pot and stuck it on the range and heated her milk the hard way. She filled two bottles with care and carried them back to the stables.

She'd never been in the stables before—she'd been

hardly anywhere in this vast, rambling castle—but the stables were unmistakable. They consisted of a vast undercover walkway with stall after stall on either side. Each stall had a horse's name above. The alleyway in front of the stalls was cobbled and the cobbles were worn with generation upon generation of boots and horseshoes.

Where were all these horses? The stalls were deserted.

Except the first stall. She peered in and found them. Raoul had located fresh hay and spread it liberally. He was sitting against the back wall, with an alpaca baby on each knee.

For a moment the sight of him took her breath away. A big man, a prince, dressed in casual clothes, dressed for the outdoors, a physician…a man with hay in his hair and with a tiny baby on each knee.

'About time,' he told her and the spell was broken—or broken a bit—and she managed to smile and go sit down beside him in the hay.

'I'm not sure how we do this,' she told him.

'I'd guess that we stick the teat end of the bottle in the mouth end of the alpaca and see what happens,' he told her.

'Gee,' she said admiringly. 'That's what a medical degree teaches you, huh?'

'That's not the half of it, lady,' he told her. 'Let's give it a try.'

So they did. And it worked.

And then it became even more unsettling, Jess decided. Sitting on the fresh-smelling hay, her shoulder just brushing the man beside her, with the babies sucking greedily at their bottles as they nestled into the knees of their human carers…

It was so domestic it was scary, Jess thought, and then she thought, yep, she was beginning to be scared. She was definitely scared. Since Dominic's death—well, ever since his diagnosis—she'd felt way out of control, and now…it was as if there was an edge somewhere really close, and she was about to go into free-fall.

They didn't speak. Jess couldn't think of a thing to say, and it seemed Raoul was no smarter. The tiny alpacas drank most of their bottles, but it had been a huge day for the baby alpacas. As the level of the bottles dropped, their drinking slowed, and as the last of the milk drained away the babies drifted off to sleep.

They were twins. They gave each other comfort. Their mother had never fed them, they knew humans as the source of their food and they had each other. So, fed and warm, they nestled together without fear on the soft hay and slept.

'I guess we can leave them,' Jess said and her voice sounded funny. That edge was definitely closer.

Raoul had risen and was holding out his hand to pull her up. She took it, uncertainly. 'I'll bring Edouard down later to introduce him to them,' he said. He tugged her to her feet and she rose and was suddenly too close.

Far too close.

'I guess we should go tell the others what we've done,' Raoul said, but he didn't move.

'I guess.'

'Jess, I want to thank you.'

'No thanks needed.' Her voice had fallen to a whisper. She didn't know why, but it had. Stupid, stupid, stupid.

Step away from the edge.

'Without you...'

'Without me you would have found someone else.'

'No one else,' he said, softly. He was already holding one of her hands. Suddenly he was holding the other. He was looking down into her eyes, he was tugging her against him—and then, without her willing it, without her knowing exactly how it had happened—or why—he was kissing her.

She didn't want to kiss Raoul Louis d'Apergenet. She did not!

Who was she kidding? She wanted to kiss Raoul Louis d'Apergenet more than anything—anyone!—in the world. He was lowering his mouth onto hers, she was opening her lips to him and it felt the most natural, the most wonderful thing that she'd ever done in her life.

It felt as if she had found her home.

This man could kiss! The sensations she'd experienced during their wedding kiss came flooding back. Raoul was right for her. He was the other half of her whole. They fitted together perfectly, and he filled a need in her that she hadn't known she had—that she hadn't known existed. Now it felt so good, so right, that to tear herself away was unthinkable.

He smelled wonderful. New-mown hay, milk, baby alpaca and…and Raoul.

He felt wonderful.

He tasted just fine.

She could forget herself in this man's arms, she thought blissfully, and promptly did.

For Jess, the last two years had been a blur of misery and despair. She'd emerged at the end of the struggle for Dom's life thinking she could never again feel life above the grey fog she lived in.

But in these few days…no, in these last few hours the fog had been blasted clear. There was life outside her fog. Life was waiting. Raoul was waiting.

But he was no longer waiting. Raoul was claiming her for life. Life was…beginning.

And she gloried in the sensation. Her fingers were entwined in his hair, claiming him, deepening the kiss. She felt her body respond, aroused as it had never been aroused, wanting as it had never wanted…

Raoul.

How did he make her feel like this? She didn't know and she wasn't asking questions. For now there was only this moment, this sensation of pure pleasure, of aching need fulfilled, and the feeling that it was reciprocated.

This man was her husband.

'My wife,' he murmured in her ear and it felt right.

This was the start of the rest of her life?

His hands were on her blouse, unfastening the buttons. She wasn't objecting. Why would she? His hands were rough and warm and tender on her breasts and she wanted this as much as he wanted it.

Raoul. Her husband.

'We don't have witnesses,' she murmured and she felt him smile.

'Excellent.'

Excellent was good. Excellent was...well, excellent. No more questions.

Or maybe just the one. His hands were moving lower, caressing her hips. She felt herself ache with pleasure and with need, and she knew...she knew that the question that had to be asked must be asked now. Now!

'Um...do we have protection?'

That gave pause. He pulled back, enough to look down into her eyes—and he groaned.

'Hell.'

Hell indeed.

'Hay's prickly anyway, my love,' she whispered, trying to ignore the jolt of dismay that she felt run through her whole body. But she couldn't ignore it. Something had happened to her here that was unfathomable. Every inch of her was screaming that she was married—joined—and they should begin their marriage right now. Protection or not. In this sweet-smelling hay, with sleeping babies beside them...

Babies. Not! They both thought the same thing at the same time and their bodies jerked apart a whole half-inch.

'Hell.' It was a deeper groan, heartfelt. Raoul raked

his hair in dismay, but he took her into his arms again, tender and yet proprietorial. Claiming his own. Claiming his wife?

'I guess it does matter,' he whispered into her hair.

'It surely does.' Her words sounded firm. She wasn't the least bit firm inside though. She was very, very wobbly. 'If you think I'm going back to Australia pregnant…'

'Do you need to go back to Australia?'

It was her turn to pause then. To pull back. To stare at his face and try to read his eyes.

'Of course I need to go.'

'We could wait and see if this marriage could work.'

Another pause. Everything seemed to still. What was he saying? 'Yeah?' she managed, but it was a squeak.

'Love, we need to think…'

But there was no time to think. Not now. 'Uncle Raoul!' It was a child's high-pitched call from outside the stables.

Edouard.

'Raoul?'

That was Louise.

Jess stiffened. She pulled away a little more, brushing hay from her clothes, from her hair.

Raoul stayed where he was, watching her.

'Jess…'

'This is nonsense.' Of course it had to be nonsense. A fairy tale with a happy ending. 'What…what a thing to say.'

'I'm stuck here,' he told her. 'It might not be so bad. We could work things out.'

'You want to be stuck here with a wife?'

'It'd be better than being alone,' he told her and she stared at him, astounded.

'Are you proposing?'

'I might be.'

'Well, don't,' she snapped. 'Of all the romantic—'

'Jess, we both know that romance doesn't work.'

'Doesn't it?' She was glaring at him, her glare on high beam. 'You'd know. Of course you'd know. A thousand women...'

'Hey, I was joking about the thousand women.'

'And I was fooling around when I let you kiss me,' she snapped.

'You were kissing back.'

'I was being kind.' She glowered. 'You've got hay stuck in your hair.'

'I need to be compromised.'

'By sleeping on the settee in my bedroom. Not by rolling in the hay.'

'It'd be more fun rolling in the hay.'

He was laughing. The rat was laughing. 'Cut it out, Raoul,' she managed. 'Edouard is looking for us.'

'So he is. You want to hide?'

Enough. Raoul had dragged a bale of hay into the stables to make a bed for the alpacas. He'd spread out most of the bale but there was a sizeable chunk still intact, pressed together in a square. He stood, smiling softly at her, inviting her to seduction—and she cracked.

She lifted the square of hay and threw it. Hard.

So when Edouard and his grandmother reached the door of their stall they found a glowering bride and a bridegroom who was covered in a cloud of hay.

CHAPTER NINE

'SO TELL us what's happening.'

They were all settled in the hay: Raoul, Jess, Louise and Edouard, and Henri. Louise had taken one look at the incoherent pair and had called Henri for back-up. 'Because I can't get any sense out of them and maybe you can.' Now she was demanding answers.

Only Edouard wasn't interested. The little boy had Sebastian in one hand and he was gently stroking Balthazar's nose with the other. He was totally entranced. Leaving his elders to sort out the non-important stuff.

'The phone's going crazy,' Louise told them. 'Henri tells me you sneaked out at dawn…'

'We didn't sneak,' Raoul objected but Jess cast him a withering look.

'Yes, we did.' She was in the mood for contradiction. What had he said? Try marriage because it's better than being stuck here alone? He had to be kidding.

'We snook,' she told Louise and Henri. 'And it worked. We're legally married.'

Louise stared from one to the other in disbelief. 'You can't be.'

'We are,' she said. 'Dopey as it sounds, I've married your son.'

'Hey, who's dopey?' Raoul complained. He was smiling at her with a smile she didn't understand—and didn't trust a bit. 'It's not dopey. The more I think about it, the more I'm deciding that marriage is a good idea.'

'For today.'

'Or maybe a bit longer,' Raoul said.

Yeah, right.

'Momentarily,' she said, in the firmest voice she could muster. 'It's a momentary marriage so you can keep Edouard safe.'

'Momentary?' Louise looked really confused.

'Oh, the marriage can last,' she told her, casting a repressive glance at her bridegroom. 'But the bride goes back to Australia tomorrow.'

Louise stared from Jess to Raoul and back again, her face saying she didn't believe a word of it. She turned to Henri, doubtful. 'Is this true?'

'I've been talking to Monsieur Luiten on the telephone,' Henri told her. 'It's true.'

'When were you talking to Monsieur Luiten?'

'Just now.'

'While Edouard and I were searching.' She cast him a look of disbelief. 'You knew of this?'

'It was Henri's suggestion,' Jess told Louise.

'Hey, the marriage was your suggestion,' Raoul objected. 'Mama, I was propositioned, just like that. Marry me, she said, and what was a chivalrous prince supposed to do?'

'You really have married Jessie,' Louise said. She stared down at Jess's hand—at the plaited band of ancient gold. 'It's my mother's ring.'

'I couldn't find anything else at short notice,' Raoul said apologetically. 'I hope you don't mind.'

'Of course I don't mind,' Louise whispered. 'Why would I mind? My mother's ring to be used for this…'

'Hey,' Jess said, suddenly even more uneasy than she was. 'It's not a real marriage.'

'Not…'

'It is a real marriage,' Raoul told them. 'Forever and ever. That's what we agreed on, isn't it, Jess?'

'Yes, but not together,' she managed. He was too near, she decided. Too close. Too…Raoul. 'As I said, I'm going back to Australia.'

'I am very, very confused,' Louise complained. 'You're going back to Australia—but you're married. A momentary marriage. Would you mind starting at the beginning and telling me just what is going on?'

So they told her. Or Raoul told her and Jess listened while he outlined the very sensible reasons they'd decided to marry. She listened while he talked about their early-morning marriage ceremony, of Monsieur Luiten's assurances that all would be right with their world. She listened while he described the advent of the twins into their lives—how the news of their marriage had become public. She listened while he finished off with,

'But I've been thinking, Mama. If we can persuade Jess to stay on for a bit…it'd be so much easier.'

Easier? Easier for whom?

'It'd be good for the little one,' Henri said with a glance across to Edouard. Only it was an uneasy glance. Henri at least had realised there might be problems.

Of course there were problems, Jess thought savagely. She watched as Henri's eyes turned doubtfully to her and she thought, This old man has more sensitivity than his master.

They were all looking at Edouard now—and there was the crux of the matter.

Edouard.

Of course it'd be good for Edouard, Jess thought. Of course it would be easier. She looked at the little boy, who was stroking the tiny alpacas as if he couldn't believe they were real, and she knew that she could make a difference to this child. She could love him to bits. She could...

She couldn't. Because every time she looked at him...

He wasn't Dominic.

'It's not fair of you to ask me to do this,' she said, the laughter and the craziness of the morning suddenly dissipating as if it had never been. 'Raoul, this was never in the deal.'

'You've lost a child,' Henri said on a note of discovery and Jess winced. How...

'My wife felt like that, too, once,' Henri said. 'When our only baby was stillborn. And the Princess Louise...' He glanced across at Raoul's mother. 'When Lisle was born she couldn't bear to look at little girls who could skip or run or play. It's a barrier.'

'What are we talking about?' Louise said, still confused, but Jess had had enough.

'It seems Henri's figured it out. I've told Raoul but he doesn't believe me,' she said, savagely into the stillness. 'Raoul, I've done the best I can for you all. It's the best I'm capable of and I can give no more. And now...' once more she pushed herself to her feet '...I need to be alone for a bit,' she told them. 'If you'll excuse me, it's been a long morning. I need to rest.'

'Of course, my dear,' Louise said, immediately contrite. 'You were only out of bed for the first time yesterday, and now this. Raoul, take Jess to—'

'I'll take myself.' She was sounding ungracious but she couldn't help herself. She'd reached the end.

'What are the alpacas' names?' Edouard asked into the stillness, and at least here was an easy question.

'Balthazar and Whatshername.'

'Balthazar,' Louise said, and her face turned to Raoul, wondering. 'You called him Balthazar for Lisle.'

'Whatshername is a funny name for a baby,' Edouard said.

'It's Australian for I Don't Know What,' Henri told him, looking from Raoul to Louise and deciding no one else was going to answer.

Edouard screwed his nose up, disapproving. In his opinion I Don't Know What was obviously not a fine name.

'Is it a girl or a boy?'

'It's a girl,' Jess managed.

'What's a better Australian name for a baby?' Edouard demanded.

'Matilda,' she told him, and he was pleased to approve.

'That's better than I Don't Know What.'

But Jess was already backing out of the stall door.

'Jess, let me come with you.' Raoul glanced uncertainly at his mother—who looked as if she was about to burst into tears—but he rose and made as if to follow. Jess put out a hand in a gesture to stop him. 'I've made a mess of things,' he told her.

'You haven't made a mess of things,' she told him, as firmly as she was able. 'You married me as you intended and you've made Edouard safe. There was no intention for us to take it further.'

'But—'

'I'm not taking it further, Raoul,' she told him. 'Get used to it.'

'Let her go, Raoul,' Louise told him. 'Can't you see that she's had enough?'

Good call, she thought. She'd definitely had enough.

'Stay with your family, Raoul,' she told him. 'You have lots of things to plan.' She looked uncertainly down at the twins. 'I think you also need to find an alpaca expert to tell you the proper way to raise these.'

'But you—'

'They're nothing to do with me now, Raoul,' she told him, in a voice that was strangely firm in the face of what she was feeling. 'I'm going home.'

* * *

She stayed in her apartment for the rest of the day.

Louise was right when she'd reminded her that she'd not been long out of bed. She'd had six days in bed after the accident. The night before had been her first time out of bed, and her knees were decidedly wobbly.

Everything about her was wobbly. Her head was spinning. Every time she stood up the walls seemed to wobble, and she decided the best thing she could do was bury her head under the pillows and will the world to go away.

Only of course it didn't. It receded a little but that was all.

Henri appeared with a tray and stayed to make sure she ate her lunch. 'Because if I don't, Raoul will, and I have a feeling you need a little time out from His Highness,' Henri told her. He made no further comment but Jess could see that he understood.

He was a nice old man, she thought as she forced herself to eat her soup and sandwiches. What had he said? He and his wife had lost a baby, too?

There was tragedy everywhere, she thought bleakly. She just had to get home. Get away from it.

Start again?

Her head was spinning. Henri cleared her dishes, she hauled her pillows back into place—and to her surprise, she slept.

It wasn't just the emotions of the morning. Seven days ago she'd been in a terrible car crash and her body was still demanding recovery time.

She woke and there was another meal tray beside

her. This time it had been brought by Louise. She was seated in the armchair by the bed waiting for her...her daughter-in-law, to wake.

'Raoul wanted to bring you this,' she said, smiling down at her. 'But Henri and I have teamed up against him. He's a very overpowering man, my son.'

'Very overpowering,' she agreed. She pushed herself up on the pillows, shoving away the sensation that she was still sleeping. 'I'm sorry.' She stared down at the dinner tray in astonishment. 'Have I slept all afternoon?'

'We're having dinner early,' Louise said apologetically. 'Raoul's trying to organise something for this evening. But you certainly have been sleeping. Maybe you needed to.'

'Maybe I did,' she said slowly. 'It was some morning.'

Louise smiled, gently sympathetic. 'You know, I always wanted a royal wedding,' she told her. 'My parents were minor royalty. They'd had a wedding with all the pomp and ceremony possible so it was what I dreamed of, too. Bridesmaids and flower-girls, pageboys, coaches, white horses, heads of state pouring into the country...' She handed over Jess's dinner plate and she sighed. 'When I was seventeen it seemed like a fairy tale, and when the prince proposed I couldn't believe my luck.'

'It must have been wonderful,' Jess said softly and Louise grimaced.

'It certainly was. A magical wedding. Followed by

a nightmare marriage.' She hesitated. 'I'm thinking that maybe you and Raoul can have the opposite.'

Jess stilled. 'Pardon?'

'You know, he thinks you're wonderful.'

'Raoul does?'

'Of course Raoul does.'

'There's no of course about it,' she muttered, slicing into a piece of steak as though it were Raoul himself. 'I didn't know the man until yesterday. Now I've married him and he's calmly suggesting I stay here forever.' She eyed the piece of steak on her fork and bit. 'You know,' she added, addressing the steak, 'if I agreed to his crazy proposal, I wouldn't be the least surprised if he stayed playing husband for just as long as it took to get Marcel sorted, and then he disappeared right back to Somalia.'

'It wouldn't surprise me either,' Louise said and once again Jess's implements stilled.

'You're not seriously suggesting I take over here? Princess Regent or somesuch?'

'You see,' Louise said—apologetically, 'I'm not sure what else we can do.'

'Get on without me,' she told her. This steak was delicious. If she could stop thinking about marriage— stop thinking about Raoul—she could really enjoy it. 'Like you all intended to get on without Sarah.'

'Sarah would have stayed here.'

'As Edouard's step-mother? From what I've heard about her, I doubt it.'

'No, it would have been a mess,' Louise agreed. 'But if you leave now it'll be a bigger mess.'

'I don't see it.'

'Raoul doesn't commit,' Louise said, almost sadly, and now it was Jess's turn to sigh. She laid down her cutlery and turned to her mother-in-law.

'Why are you telling me this?'

'You're his wife.' She hesitated a little more but then continued. 'You know, I've never told anyone this. But I thought…you really are married to him. It's not betrayal for a woman to talk about her son to his wife.'

'I'm a wife in name only.'

'You're his wife.' Louise lifted the knife and fork and placed them firmly back in Jess's hands. 'Eat. And listen. I intend to tell you, like it or not.'

'But—'

'Listen.'

So Jess listened. Short of throwing the tray and Louise out of the room, she had no choice at all, and, looking at Louise's face, she knew there was a need here that had been growing for a long time.

'I've worried about him for years,' Louise said, echoing her thoughts, and Jess decided there was nothing for it but to attack her steak and remain silent.

'My husband and I had a dreadful marriage,' Louise said softly. 'Royalty married to youth. It didn't work. My husband took Jean-Paul as his son and heir, and he doted on him. Then six years later the twins were born, and Lisle was not…perfect. My husband demanded perfection. Maybe he could have loved Raoul, but of course Raoul was inseparable from his sister. From the time Raoul could understand, his father was trying to split him from Lisle, and Raoul was a fighter. He fought his father. He fought me when I tried to intervene. And then…' She hesitated while Jess ate two delicious little potatoes with parsley butter. 'Then I finally took the twins away. It was breaking my heart that I couldn't stay in contact with Jean-Paul. I was so bitter about marriage. So maybe…maybe Raoul was brought up thinking that marriage and relationships were doomed. Independence was everything.' She bit her lip and looked down at her hands. 'Maybe I've done even more damage. And maybe the only way for the damage to be undone is for someone to stay.'

'You mean for me to stay.'

'If you've the courage.'

'I don't have the courage,' she said flatly. 'I can't look at Edouard without hurting. I've been really good at failed relationships in the past. And if Raoul thinks he can dump his responsibilities onto me and go back to saving the world—'

'I'm sure he doesn't mean that.'

'I'll bet he does.'

Louise rose, but she was wringing her hands, her fingers entangled and frantic. 'I know. This is so unfair. But if you go…'

'Then you'll work something out. And you'll be better off than if we hadn't married.'

'I know that. So it's quite unfair to ask for more.'

'Yes,' Jess said flatly. She was feeling a little ill and she laid down her knife and fork for the last time.

There was a dessert by her dinner plate—a concoction of meringue and berries. It looked amazing.

She'd completely lost her appetite.

'I've done all I can,' she told Louise, gazing at it in distaste. 'Enough. Please don't ask more.'

She didn't see anyone then until after dusk. She lay in bed, desultorily reading magazines Louise had thoughtfully provided. She made a couple of phone calls to confirm what she needed to do tomorrow. She tried not to think about what was happening in the palace without her.

She tried not to think about Raoul.

Then, as the last of the light faded from the windows and she was thinking about the impossibility of going to sleep, there was a knock.

'Come in,' she called and Raoul opened the door.

Or…Prince Raoul.

He was wearing some sort of uniform, and what a uniform! It was a dress suit, of a fabric so blue it was almost black, and its magnificence took her breath away. Medals blazed across his chest. Rows of gold braid and tassels adorned his arms. A purple sash with gold edging slashed across his chest and at his side hung a jewel-encrusted sword.

He looked…breathtaking.

'If you laugh I'm going to have to kill you,' he told her conversationally. 'Can I come in?'

'You look amazing,' she managed. This was crazy. Prince descending to the peasant quarters—like something straight out of Cinderella. Had Cinders ever been caught snoozing in bed? she wondered. She shoved *World Celebrities* under the pillow. Who needed pictures when she had the real thing?

'I look ridiculous,' he told her, still discomfited.

'Ridiculous is hardly the word I'd use,' she told him. With his dark skin, his beautifully groomed hair, his deep, dark eyes creased into a rueful smile—and that uniform… No, *ridiculous* definitely didn't spring to mind.

'If the guys in my med team could see me now…'

'If the girls in your med team could see you now, they'd swoon,' she told him.

'Are you swooning?'

'No, but I…' She took a deep breath. 'I don't do swooning.'

'You're past it?'

'Something like that.'

He appeared to consider—and then he smiled, moving on. 'Maybe. Maybe not,' he said enigmatically. 'Meanwhile you've got your own dressing up to do. My mother was planning on helping but the veterinarian's here to give lessons in the care of baby alpacas, so she and Edouard are down in the stables.'

'Right,' she said cautiously. 'So…'

'So we have official photographers arriving in half an hour,' he told her. 'Plus the Press.' He turned aside and called to someone obviously further down the hall. 'Marie? Her Highness is awake. We can start.'

Her Highness. That would be her?

A little dark woman appeared by Raoul's side. She

was beaming and beaming, and her arms were laden with…

A gown? Surely this wasn't a gown?

But it seems it was. 'Marie's here to help you dress,' Raoul told her. His smile deepened as he sympathised with her confusion. 'Unless you want to get your official photographs taken in what you're wearing?'

'Hey.' She tried to make her dizzy mind think. 'What is this?'

'You agreed on tonight, yes?'

'Tonight.'

'We need to stay together,' he told her, his smile fading. 'You remember?'

'Y-yes, but…'

'Well, tonight starts now,' he told her. 'Mama and I agreed we should get the entire thing over and done with. Marie's here with a formal gown for official photographs and for the small ceremony of blessing we've planned. We have a cosmetician and a hairdresser and a bevy of reporters waiting. As soon as you're decent we'll let the hordes in and they can interview you.'

To say she was confused was an understatement. 'But—'

'It's the shortest way,' he told her, still sympathetic. 'The media won't be satisfied unless they're given an official photo opportunity. The television crews want some sort of ceremony. Marcel's having apoplexy, and by not producing you we're asking for trouble. So can I ask that you be produced?'

She eyed him. She eyed his uniform.

'Like you've been produced?'

'That's right,' he told her and his smile suddenly reached out again to touch her. It did touch her. He looked absurdly handsome. Absurdly anxious?

He was as out of his depth as she was, she thought. He'd been thrown into the media spotlight with not much more warning than she had had.

Tonight he needed her, and she'd agreed.

She'd give him tonight.

'Fine,' she said, and it was as if she'd switched on a light. Relief washed over his face, lighting places she hadn't realised were in shadow.

'Really?'

He thought he'd messed it up, she realised, watching his face. He'd thought that his crazy proposal to extend this marriage had somehow jeopardised her agreement to do what was needed tonight.

'Of course, really.'

'Jess.' It was a soft word, an utterance of her name—but he might as well have kissed her. He smiled at her and she felt...

He felt, too. He seemed to drag his eyes away, and when he spoke again his voice was strained.

But he was back to being businesslike. Maybe thankfully? 'OK, Marie.' He motioned to the gown Marie was carrying. 'This is a gown Mama wore for state occasions,' he told her. 'It was worn by my grandmother and her mother before her. Because of its historical significance it's one of the few things of

Mama's that my father didn't destroy. Mama's sure it'll fit. You're practically the same size as she is.'

'But…'

'Jess, it's a state occasion,' he told her. 'A royal marriage.' He smiled at her, his eyes holding, reassuring, teasing. 'If I have to look like something on a biscuit tin, I don't see why you don't join me.'

She stared. He was laughing at her.

No. He was laughing with her. There was a difference.

She loved it.

'You don't look like something on a biscuit tin,' she managed. Humour was the way to go here, she decided. If he could laugh then she could, too. It was a close call though. Could she laugh without toppling into hysteria?

'Maybe I'd say you looked a bit tinnish if you weren't wearing a sword,' she told him. 'But I'll never describe a man wearing a sword as a tin-lid decoration. It's a rule I've stuck to in the past, and I dare say it'll serve me well in the future.'

'I dare say it will,' he said faintly. He was responding to her laughter with a look of pure admiration that did her anxious insides the world of good. And then he moved on.

'OK, Princess Jessica,' he told her. 'Tin lids or not, we're in this together. Shall we start being decorative now?'

Playing dressing-up had nothing on this.

The dress itself was enough to take her breath away.

It was a dress one was wedged into rather than slipped on, she thought. Without a body, the dress would stand up by itself.

The rich silver brocade was heavily embroidered with crimson and gold. It was cut like the robes she'd seen of mediaeval princesses. The bodice, with its low square neckline, flattened her breasts with its heavy fabric, but at the same time it somehow accentuated her breasts' soft swell. The sleeves fell to her finger-tips, close-fitting from her shoulders and widening below the elbows, with a circlet of softer fabric at the wrists falling almost to her knees. The vast, embroidered skirt was rich and full, touching the floor at the front and sweeping to a glorious train of gold and silver at the back.

There was a brilliant crimson dragon embroidered on the train.

'It's the family emblem,' Raoul told her, and she cast him a look of disbelief.

'Think of it as a family pet. And you're part of our family.'

'Then let's change the family emblem to a small, custard-yellow porrywiggle,' she retorted. 'Because that's the way I'm feeling.'

He grinned—but there was no backing out now. Marie was admitting the world to admire her. And they were admiring. In moments she was surrounded by reporters and cameramen, and they were aiming straight at her.

For Jess the sensation was so unbelievable she sought refuge in humour.

'I need one of those pointy caps,' she said, staring at herself in the mirror as the final adjustments were made to her train, to her face, to her hair, in readiness for the official photographer. 'Like you see on princesses in comic books.'

Silence.

'My wife likes to laugh,' Raoul told the assemblage.

Jess bit her lip. Uh-oh. Wasn't humour the way to go, then?

She was his wife for a night. His dignity needed her to behave.

But he looked reproving, she thought suddenly. Reproving? If he thought she was going to buckle down and be a tin-lid...

'Well, if I can't have a cap I guess I'll just have to do without,' she said mournfully. 'I guess, as we intend to stay in tonight—dear—then I'll make do with this old outfit and a bare head. After all—' she gave Raoul her kindest smile '—it's not as if you're dressed for going out.'

Raoul's eyes creased in disbelief—and then into stunned admiration, and the assembled media stared. There was a long pause as if no one could believe what they were hearing.

And then—finally—there was laughter. Tentative at first, and then deeply appreciative.

Jess was used to reporters. Her designs were known around the world and she'd learned to manipulate the media for her own ends. Now she chose to answer exactly what she wanted to answer. Any other questions she ignored with the deftness born of practice.

Had she a family in Australia?

'Yes.'

She'd been married before?

'Yes.'

Then it got trickier.

'You've had a child?' someone asked. 'Our sources in Australia have done some fast research and they say your child died of leukaemia.'

'Dominic died, yes.' She paused, and then said softly, as if speaking personally to each and every one of the assembled reporters, 'That's why I believe family is so important. It's why it's so important that Prince Edouard can stay with his uncle and his grandmother, rather than his distant cousin. I'm sure every person in this country would agree, and this marriage makes that possible.'

They loved her.

They thought she was fantastic, Raoul thought as, questions completed, they made their way to the tiny palace chapel. Here their marriage would be blessed in a ceremony designed—hastily—to give the people their only chance to meet their princess.

This was right.

But it needed to continue.

If she stayed it'd be so much easier, he thought. Jessie's hand was resting on his arm as they made their way through the long corridors. Cameras were working at full speed. She wasn't flinching.

She was wonderful.

He could do this if he had Jessie by his side.

And Jess was alone. Back in Australia she had no one, and the thought made his gut wrench. She had no family and she'd lost her child. She was going home to the grey fog he could sense had been overwhelming her, and he knew that the fog was waiting to engulf her again.

But here she'd lifted his own bleakness, and she'd smiled and entranced the media and she'd brought happiness to a place that could give her happiness in return. She could set up her design centre here, he thought, his mind racing. He'd pay to bring any staff she needed over and maybe they could build Waves up even bigger than it was now. This country had the best yarns and the best cloth. Why not the best designer?

It could work, he thought, and the more the idea whirled through his mind, the better it looked. Jess would be surrounded by her staff—and by her family. Louise would love her. Edouard would love her.

And he…

In time maybe even he…

She was laughing at something one of the reporters had said. He glanced down at the smiling woman on his arm and he felt the growing realisation that things were changing very fast.

Maybe he already did love her, he conceded, but the nebulous idea was immense and overwhelming and even plain damned scary.

But sending Jess home alone seemed even more scary.

She had to stay. She must. It was a brilliant idea and not to try it seemed crazy.

So… He had this night to persuade her, he thought. This night the marriage was supposed to be consummated.

This night she had to agree to marry him in earnest.

The tiny ceremony devised to introduce Jess to the country, to the people, was a simple ceremony of blessing.

It shouldn't have the power to move her.

But she stood at the end of the aisle and the old priest stood before them in his faded vestments. A soft smile lingered behind his kindly old eyes. He murmured the words of blessing as if he meant every one of them—blessing this marriage forever—and she was definitely moved.

Raoul's hand held hers. The warmth of him, the strength…the look of pride on his face…

For this moment, this mock-marriage seemed almost real.

And for this moment she almost had a family. Louise was in the front pew, holding Edouard. The little boy had his arms around his grandmother's neck. His time with Louise in the alpacas' stall had obviously made him decide this lady was someone he might trust. The ghastly Cosette didn't appear to be missed at all.

Raoul and Louise had made a tiny beginning to give this needful child a family, Jess thought. A family…

It made her want to cry.

Raoul's hand held her still and as she looked up at him he smiled gently, reassuringly into her eyes. She was wearing his ring. Almost she could believe in fairy tales, she thought. She could believe that this was her prince and she was loved and she was walking into a happy ending.

Just keep remembering midnight, she told herself fiercely, desperately. The pumpkins will happen sooner than you think.

And somehow she managed to keep herself in control, even when, at the end of the blessing, Raoul turned and kissed her.

This was no kiss of passion. It was a kiss of gratitude, for all the world to see.

'Thank you, Jessica,' he told her, and his voice was firm enough for all who were present to hear, and through the microphone for all who were glued to television sets across the country to hear. 'Thank you from me and from Crown Prince Edouard and from my mother. And thank you from my country, from my people. We all love you and you'll be in our hearts forever.'

Yeah, right. Nice speech, Raoul, she thought, frantically fighting back stupid tears that meant nothing.

Bring on the pumpkins. Now.

There was a reception—of sorts. So many people, gathered at short notice to make this strange mock-marriage official.

There were so many people that the night was a blur. She smiled and shook hands and curtsied as if she'd been bred to it. She moved from one dignitary to another, being introduced, being questioned, making small talk. Raoul assisted as much as he could but the attention was all on her.

'You've done enough,' Raoul told her at last but she shook her head. She could do this. One night…

But Raoul had support. 'Jess cannot stay any longer,' Louise declared and she didn't say it to Jess. She said it to the room at large. Louise had left the reception briefly to put Edouard to bed and she'd come back to see Jess wilting. Louise, of all of them, had the most experience of being royalty. She, too, had been a royal bride.

'She's not well enough for more,' she declared now. 'Raoul, it's time to take your bride to her bed.'

There was a pause throughout the room as somehow everyone caught Louise's words.

And then there was a cheer.

Raoul looked down at his bride and he smiled.

She didn't smile back. She was close to being overwhelmed here and her autopilot seemed to be shutting down.

'Can I take you to bed, Princess Jessica?'

'If you must,' she murmured, thoroughly confused, not just by the situation but also by the tenderness she read in her husband's eyes. This whole situation was fantastic, and the idea that the assemblage was cheering the royal couple to bed was ridiculous. And that Raoul should look at her like this…

Back to basics, Jessica, she told herself. Get some control here.

'Fine,' she murmured, so softly that only Raoul could hear. 'Or almost fine. You're not taking me to bed. You're taking me to the bedroom. That's it.' She hesitated and smiled around at the cheering audience before starting to whisper again. 'But it's bedroom door only, Your Highness. You stop at the settee. I'll make it the rest of the way by myself.'

He smiled, his eyes gently teasing. 'I'm glad you agree, my lovely bride.' And then, before she knew what he was about, he swept her up into his arms. Her glorious dress hung about her. He stood among the gathering, holding her, claiming her, laughing down into her eyes.

A prince, laying claim to his bride.

'You'll have to excuse us,' he told the assemblage and there were more cheers and laughter.

Vaguely Jess was aware of Marcel, glaring at her with hatred from the corner of the room. But it didn't matter. How could anything matter when Raoul was holding her like this?

Or maybe it did matter. Maybe Marcel's awfulness was the simple reason why Raoul was holding her like this.

But Raoul was still speaking. 'You need to excuse us,' Raoul said again, and the whole room hushed. 'I need to take my bride to bed.'

CHAPTER TEN

HE DIDN'T take her to her bedroom.

They reached the turn in the corridor she knew and he turned left and not right.

'Hey,' she said and wriggled, and his hold on her tightened.

'Yes, my darling?'

'I am not your darling,' she told him.

In reply he stooped and kissed her, effectively silencing her. Then, with his mouth only half an inch from hers, he whispered, 'Hush, my love. We're being followed.'

'Followed?'

She glanced back over his shoulder. No easy feat this, glancing over the shoulder of the man who was carrying her. It involved a certain amount of contortion as he wasn't loosening his hold and she felt a little like a minnow enveloped in a sea of embroidered satin—but somehow she did it.

There were men in the corridor behind them. Suits. There were suits following them?

'Um…who?'

'It's the Minister for the Crown,' he told her, 'and his minions.'

That jolted her. Badly.

'Please tell me they're not intending to watch,' she demanded, and he smiled.

'No. We're not in the Dark Ages.'

'Then why are they here?'

'They'll settle outside the bedroom door and check we stay together overnight.'

'Who said you're not in the Dark Ages?'

'It's better than them watching. It's a compromise and if we don't agree to their presence then our wedding may be deemed not to be consummated.' He hesitated. 'There'd be no problem if you agreed to stay forever. Jess, I'd really like you to consider the advantages. You know, there are advantages—for all of us. Resettling here, bringing your work here, having us take care of you... But if you're intent on leaving...'

For heaven's sake, what was he proposing? 'Of course I'm leaving.'

'Then Marcel will fight to have the marriage annulled. I told you this.'

'Yeah, but I didn't really believe you,' she said darkly. 'It seemed a bit of a joke. Raoul...'

'Let's just go with the flow, shall we?'

She was so confused—but how could she not *go with the flow*? When he was holding her tightly against him? When he was making her feel...?

Ridiculous?

No. Not ridiculous. But there were no words to describe how she was feeling right now.

'So where are you taking me?'

'To the bridal chamber,' he said, smiling his reassurance.

'The bridal chamber!'

'Just shut up and be appreciative,' he told her. 'You're a princess for a night. Why not lie back and enjoy it?'

'I'll stand up, thank you very much.'

'If you like.' He grinned. 'Whatever takes your fancy.'

'Raoul…'

'Yes, dear?'

'You're asking for your ears to be boxed.'

'Not in front of witnesses,' he told her. 'Let's wait until we get behind closed doors and then you can do anything to me that you want. I promise.'

Which left her speechless.

Her speechless state lasted until she reached the bridal chamber. Then she opened her mouth to speak, but discovered she was speechless all over again.

Marcel's edict that no staff work in the castle must have gone out the window the moment it was realised that Raoul was married. Now two uniformed footmen flung open a pair of ornate oak doors. They ushered the newly marrieds inside, and closed the doors behind them.

Jess tried to say thank you—and failed.

From the firm hold of her husband's arms, she gazed around and she gasped in stunned wonder.

'Christopher Columbus,' she breathed at last, and Raoul smiled. In truth, he looked more than a little gobsmacked himself. 'Raoul, put me down.'

He did—but it seemed he did so reluctantly. And she stood, but she missed the feel of his arms.

Concentrate on the room, she told herself fiercely. Concentrate on the apartment.

It was certainly worth concentrating on.

Vast and opulent, the rooms dripped with crimson velvet and white satin canopies. Huge white settees were piled with white velvet cushions. More cushions were scattered over the floor—mounds and mounds of cushions on a carpet that was so thick that the pile hid her toes.

A huge fireplace blazed out a gentle heat, warming every corner.

What else? There were balloons, glistening white and silver and tied in vast bunches with white satin ribbon. Someone must have been working here all day putting the final touches to this opulent glory.

She gazed around her in wonder. The bathroom led off to the left. There was a sunken bathtub, as big as a small swimming pool, gently steaming and infinitely inviting. The tub was in the shape of a Botticelli shell.

'That's indecent,' she said, and Raoul raised his brows and wiggled them in suggestive laughter.

'It looks pretty damned good to me,' he told her. 'And it's not indecent until we're in it. Doing stuff.'

She glared. 'Which we're not going to be.'

'Not?'

'I may just try it on my own,' she said with as much dignity as she could muster. She turned her back on her husband—and turned her attention to the bedroom.

And saw the bed.

'You could sleep a small army in that bed,' she gasped—and Raoul looked through and nodded. Gravely.

'I'd guess this must have been the troops' quarters in the past.'

'Oh, right. I can just see a whole regiment tucked up in that bed.' She couldn't suppress a smile at the thought, and some of the tension eased. A little. 'This is amazing.'

'Isn't it just,' he said, and his voice was as wondering as hers.

She turned and stared at him, surprised. 'Haven't you ever been in here?'

'Not that I can remember,' he told her. 'When I was a kid I was never allowed in this section of the palace. Henri and Mama arranged that we come here tonight. They said it was appropriate.' He stared around for a bit more in appreciation. 'I don't know about appropriate,' he told her, 'but it's pretty good, huh?'

'Um…right.'

He eyed her with caution. 'Right?'

'Right,' she said, and glowered. Somehow a glower seemed necessary. In the face of his wonder. In the face of…him. She needed weapons here, she thought. She needed all the weapons she could muster and a glower was all she had.

And sense. She had to be sensible.

'The bedroom's mine,' she told him. 'You can have the rest.'

'Don't you need access to the bathroom?'

'I'll use two feet along the far wall to get there. When you're not in it.'

'You want to build a dividing wall?' he asked, entering into the spirit of things. 'With cushions? Hey, we could divide the bath. One of us on either side of the shell. Only maybe cushions wouldn't work as a barrier.' His face fell. 'They might get soggy.'

'Don't be facetious.'

'You don't think you might be just the faintest bit paranoid?'

'I'm not paranoid. I'm just…'

'Yes?'

'Scared,' she said and the glower went out of her, just like that.

'Scared of me?' His laughter had died, too. He was looking down at her with tenderness and that was worse. It made her feel a whole lot more scared.

'Raoul, we can't do this.'

'We can't what?'

'Have a marriage.'

'No.' He put a finger under her chin, tilting her face, forcing her to look up into his eyes. 'No, we can't.' His look softened and his voice lowered. 'I don't think any real marriage is possible until we both move on from the past. I'm starting to think that maybe I'm prepared to take a risk, but you…maybe you're not ready to do that. Are you?'

'N…no.'

'Then what I suggest is this,' he told her, and he released her and turned away, seeming to search for something. 'I asked Henri to find this. I've been waiting for this for almost thirty years and...yes!'

'Yes?' she said, cautiously bemused. Her royal prince was down on his hands and knees now, delving under a huge mahogany desk by the window.

'He found it,' he said, triumphant. 'He's left it here for me. Good old Henri.'

'What?' There was an element of surrealism behind this, she thought. Bride in mediaeval gown, in truly splendid bridal chamber, watching husband in full regimentals—he was still wearing his sword!—crawling under a desk. Hauling out a huge wooden box with a hinged lid.

'It's my slot-car set,' he said and the level of satisfaction in his voice made her stare.

'Your slot-car set.'

'I turned six the day before my father kicked us out of the palace,' he told her. 'But on my sixth birthday I was given the sort of slot-car set any small boy dreams of. It's sat here untouched for nearly thirty years and you can't imagine how many times I thought of it with regret. It's dumb, I know, but one of the first things I thought of when I knew I had to come back here was this. Then tonight...I figured if we had to stay locked in here all night and you intended to be cold and distant, then I was going to get it out and use it. So I asked Henri to search the attics and see if he could find it.'

A slot-car set. It was so far away from everything she'd been thinking that she couldn't believe it. She stood and her jaw felt as if it was hitting her ankles.

But something had to be cleared up first.

'I don't intend to be cold and distant.'

'What else do you call making cushion walls in the bath?'

He was impossible. 'You really do want to play with your slot-cars?'

'What else are we going to do? Beside divide rooms with cushions.' He raised his eyebrows and grinned— a grin of pure mischief. 'Unless you've changed your mind. It is a bridal suite, after all. We can always indulge in a spot of seduction. Seduction's good.' He wiggled his eyebrows some more. Seduction at its most alluring.

He didn't know how alluring.

'Play with your slot-cars,' she told him—but she smiled. How could she not smile in the face of this man's delight?

He sighed—but he moved on. 'You can play, too, if you want,' he told her and he grinned up at her again as he hauled his box open. 'There's a blue car and a red car and two controllers. And so much road... Bridges and tunnels and everything. It's never been used. What a tragedy.' He paused. 'But maybe you're not even up to playing with slot-cars. Do you want to go into the bedroom and lock the door?'

She hesitated.

She eyed him—cautiously.

She eyed the cars coming out of their box. They'd obviously been state-of-the-art thirty years ago. They looked amazing.

The decision was suddenly easy. 'I want red,' she

declared and stooped to pick up her little red car. A Porsche. 'It's not a Lamborghini,' she said, sighing, 'but I guess the peasants have to make do with what they can get.'

He smirked. 'The blue one's a Lamborghini.'

'I knew that.'

'So why did you choose red?'

'Red's my colour.' Thoroughly distracted, thoroughly disconcerted but thoroughly intrigued, she was now kneeling on the floor, pulling things out of his magic box. They had enough roadway to go all around the room. And the bridges were amazing. 'Cool!'

'I can so see that red's your colour,' he told her, eyeing her burnished curls with appreciation. 'Blue's royal. Red's for temper. I can wear that.'

'Raoul…'

'Mm?'

She was way out of her depth and she knew it. What was she supposed to say?

She said the only thing she could think of.

'Raoul, shut up and build.'

'Yes, Your Highness.'

So they built, and they raced, and it was the craziest, funniest night that Jess could remember.

Maybe there had been great nights in the past, back in her childhood, nights where all else was forgotten in the face of pure fun, but an appalling marriage followed by tragedy had driven any such memory from her mind.

She wouldn't forget this night. This was a night to remember forever.

It took an hour to set up the track. In the face of such an intriguing challenge, Jess's exhaustion fell away. People around her at the reception, making polite conversation, appraising her as a princess, had made her feel dizzy with fatigue. But here… Here she got her second wind.

Raoul was trying to set up his complicated loop before she built her bridge. He was pinching the pieces she wanted. She'd slept this afternoon. She wasn't truly tired. Besides, how could a girl go tamely into her bedroom and close the door with such a construction happening on the other side?

She couldn't.

Especially as Raoul was here.

He'd hauled off his sash, his suit coat, his shoes, his tie and his sword. He still looked like a prince but he looked like…her prince. Yes, he was still very much a prince, she thought, and then tried hard not to think about it.

On the other hand, she was no longer a princess. She'd kicked off her sandals and taken off the great overskirt with train. She was still wearing the bodice and the silken underskirt but—after some hesitation—she'd asked Raoul to loosen the stays that were flattening her breasts. With the ties at the back unfastened, her breasts bounced up again, free. That was a crucial moment in the night. Raoul eyed the swell beneath her loosened bodice. He eyed her—and decided wisely to say nothing.

With that decision safely past, she relaxed. The tension eased.

They were free; two kids with their slot-car set.

The cars were fantastic, and the road they made was amazing; tunnels, bridges, sweeping curves that looped round and round the room. It made the racing excellent. Once the road was finished they raced in earnest. They pushed their cars to the limit, the curves making them overturn, sweep off the sides, fly off into the carpet, crash against each other...

Jess was caught up in a bubble of laughter that wouldn't go away and Raoul's rich chuckle sounded out over and over again.

'You know, those guys outside from the ministry are going to think there's something really kinky going on in here,' Jess declared as they stopped laughing for long enough to line up for their final race. They'd decided on the best of three races. Then the best of five. Then the best of seventeen. Now it was the best of forty-seven. They were twenty-three wins apiece, the tiny cars were starting to smell of burned rubber and their little engines were starting to fade.

They lined them up and counted down. Round and round flew the cars, squealing against the rails, clashing against each other, screaming into the next lap, hitting full gear, fast, faster, faster...

They hit the kerb by the bedpost. Raoul's car clipped her rear tyre. Her tiny red Porsche did a double back somersault and flew into the air.

And hit Raoul beneath the eye.

'Ouch!' He fell back against the bed, laughing so

hard he could hardly hold his hand to his face. But with his spare hand he was still gripping the controls. Pressing harder…

The crash had done its damage. His tiny blue Lamborghini slowed. It slowed still further.

It stopped six inches from the finish.

Raoul looked sideways at his opposition—and reached out a finger and pushed it over the finishing line.

'Hey.' Jess retrieved her little car, which was smoking ominously from the rear end. It was going to need major love to get it going again. 'You're not allowed to push.'

'There's no rule that says I'm not allowed to push.'

'I'll bet there is. You've won by foul means.'

'Whereas you've won by throwing a car at me,' he told her. 'You've even drawn blood. Talk about foul means.'

'Blood?' she said cautiously. 'You can't be serious.'

'It's serious.' He lifted his fingers and revealed a scratch a quarter of an inch long. 'I think it's mortal.'

She couldn't stop laughing. The room was a shambles. As a honeymoon suite, it made a great Formula One track.

'Let me see again?' she demanded and he lifted his hand away.

'I think I need plasma,' he said, mournfully. 'And I'm a doctor. I'd know. Or at least a kiss better.' He looked hopeful.

'I have a better idea. I'll stitch it,' she told him. 'You might be a doctor but I can sew!'

'Get away from me.' Still he was laughing. 'And don't distract me from what really matters. I demand complete disqualification on the grounds of attack.'

'You don't know what attack is.'

'I won,' he said smugly.

'You cheated.'

'The royal decree is that I won.'

'I'm royal, too,' she told him. 'And my royal decree is that you cheated.'

'I'm more royal than you are.'

For answer she lifted a cushion—and tossed. The big, squishy cushion fell plump against his face.

He let it fall, then eyed her with caution. He took his hand away from his face and checked his fingers. The really very minor scratch had stopped bleeding.

'I might live,' he said grudgingly.

'If you think you're getting a sympathy victory, think again. Wuss.'

'Wuss?' He lifted a cushion. 'You can't call a prince of the blood a wuss.'

'I can call a prince whinging about an infinitesimal scratch anything I want.' She eyed the cushion he was raising with a certain amount of trepidation. 'Don't you dare.'

'All's fair,' he said softly 'in love and war.'

He tossed the cushion straight at her.

She lifted her hand to ward it off. Her hand was still holding the tiny, scratched and battered racing car.

The car caught the side of the down-filled cushion—
and it ripped.

Feathers flew from one end of the room to another.

She sneezed. She was laughing so much there were
feathers going into her mouth. She was blinded by a
sea of white down.

'Where are you?' Raoul was fighting feathers, pushing them away from him, laughing as much as she
was. 'Hell, woman, I can't fight you if I can't see
you.'

He was reaching for her in the feathers.

'There are more cushions where they came from,'
she managed, spluttering. 'And you threw it.'

'So I did.'

He reached for her.

She reached for a cushion.

She reached the cushion as he reached her. He
seized her hands in his before she could lift it. He was
gripping hard, trying to keep the cushion from smack-
ing him in the face.

She was fighting him…fighting him…

'Desist, woman,' he spluttered.

And suddenly she wasn't fighting him at all.

How it happened she could never after explain. One
minute they were intent on killing each other with
cushions. The next…

There was a patch in the carpet where there was no
road, a looping curve with carpet in the centre. The
rug was piled with feathers, and that was where
they were.

He was holding her but he was no longer fighting. He was no longer defending himself from cushions.

He was pulling her against his chest, and she was sinking into him, still laughing but melting...melting into his arms as if everything that had happened in this night had been leading to this moment.

His mouth was claiming hers. His arms were holding her. He was laughing with her in a mixture of exasperation and laughter and tenderness, but the exasperation and the laughter were fading and the tenderness was growing. And with it...

With it an aching, surging need that had no hope of being denied. She was curving against his body as if she belonged, and that was how she felt.

For this moment—right now—this was her man. The vows she'd made... She'd made them as mock-vows—or she'd meant to make them as mock-vows—but her heart hadn't caught up with her head, and her heart was screaming that she'd vowed to love and honour this man for the rest of her life.

As he'd vowed to love her. No wonder then that he was claiming her as his wife and there was no way she could gainsay him.

For she wanted him as much as he wanted her. More. He was the other half of her whole. They'd joined, loved, declared their commitment before God and man, and they'd been made one.

'Raoul.' Somehow she whispered his name. Somehow.

Raoul.

Her hands were under his shirt, feeling the raw

strength of him, glorying in his masculinity. Her husband. Hers.

And he was claiming her. The last of the ties were being unfastened. Her bodice was falling away and she didn't care.

Wrong. She did care. She wanted this. This man was her husband.

Her love.

A thought. A desperate little thought, made at the outer edges of her consciousness where only the last ragged shreds of sanity prevailed, surfaced and started screaming. No. But it had to be said.

'Raoul, we can't...'

He pulled away from her then. Just a little, and he was smiling in the firelight with such tenderness that he took her breath away.

'Why can't we—my wife?'

'I... We don't have protection. Raoul, I can't...get pregnant.'

How had she found the strength to say it? She didn't know but it was out. And she caught her breath in dismay.

She wanted him. Oh, she wanted him.

Where was the nearest convenience store to this place?

But there was no need. He was turning her in his arms, cradling her, holding her close but gesturing to something by the bedroom door.

On a hall stand there was a tiny bundle of things that looked like golden coins.

'This is a bridal chamber,' he told her, his voice

husky with tenderness and with passion. 'It comes supplied.'

She gasped. She tried to work up indignation.

She failed. 'How…how…?' she stammered. Then, 'If they've been sitting there since the last marriage in this place—'

He silenced her with a kiss. When he drew back his eyes were even darker, more intense, loving her with his smile. 'Henri told me he'd put them in here personally this afternoon,' he told her. 'Just in case.'

'Well, good old Henri,' she said—trying to make her voice dry. Trying not to let her voice crack with emotion.

'He is good,' Raoul told her, his dark eyes flaring with passion. 'He's wonderful. But he's not as wonderful as you, my love.' His voice lowered then, and it was suddenly husky with passion. 'You know, I've never thought I could feel like I do now. All the decisions I made after Lisle's death, that I couldn't love anyone… Jess, I thought that I couldn't love, because to love and lose again would break my heart. But I'm falling so hard for you. This love thing… Any minute I'm going to be so irrevocably tied that to lose you would tear me apart. I intend to hold you to me forever. Please God, forever.'

'Oh, Raoul…'

It was too much. She was so close to tears, and all she could do was stare at him with eyes that were lost. Was he saying he loved her?

'But you've lost, too, my love, and a child,' he said softly and she knew he could see her pain. 'And your loss is so much more recent—more raw than mine. The leap you're making here now… I know how brave it is. For you to love me…'

What was he saying? 'I don't… I can't…'

'You do and you can,' he said softly and he kissed her long and hard, so deeply that she knew his words were absolute truth. She loved him. Oh, yes, she loved him.

And did that love betray her love for Dominic?

She didn't know. She couldn't think straight. She couldn't think at all. Not when he was smiling at her. Not when he was loving her, holding her as the most precious thing in the world.

He was her husband. Raoul.

'And now, my beautiful bride, my princess…my love,' he whispered, 'would you like your true wedding setting to be the troop bed beyond? Or would you like your wedding night to be spent between the bridge and the second tunnel of the world's best racing track?'

There was no need to answer.

She was right between the bridge and the second tunnel of the world's best racing track.

She took his beloved face in her hands, she drew him into her. Her doubts about her baby son disappeared—to be faced at some time in the future but not now. Please…not now.

For tonight there was only Raoul.

CHAPTER ELEVEN

HAPPINESS lasted until the hour before dawn.

At some time during this truly extraordinary night they'd moved. The bed made for an army had some very real advantages—like sheets—against the alternative of odd pieces of slot-car set digging in their spines. Raoul had carried his bride there at last, and some time long after that they'd slept.

But in the hour before dawn she woke.

She lay, curved into the warmth of her husband's body. She listened to his soft breathing, she felt his heartbeat, and she knew that here she could find a home.

But could she? Too much had happened too fast for this to seem like a happy ending. Too much had happened for her to take it in and with the first weak light of morning came the slivers of doubt. The fog edged back.

Could she stay here?

Last night she'd melted into him, yet how much of a considered choice had it been? What did she know of him and this whole surreal situation she'd landed herself in?

In this hour before dawn the doubts flooded back in force.

This was a strange and enigmatic man. He was a doctor, yet she'd seen nothing of his medicine. He was a prince, though she knew nothing of his country.

She'd known this man for two days. Could she spend the rest of her life beside him?

Yes, her heart was saying, but in the coldness before dawn there was room for her head to work as well.

Dominic's ashes were back in Australia and the ink was barely dry on his death certificate.

And she had an appointment.

Yesterday she'd rung a business acquaintance—the woman who organised the export of her yarns. Claire lived in Vesey and it had been Claire who'd organised her initial itinerary. Jess scarcely knew her but Claire's business depended on Jess's custom and yesterday it had seemed time to call in favours.

Claire knew all about what had happened to her—by now all the country did. She'd sounded astounded and sympathetic, but above all she'd been business-like. If Jess wanted to get back to Australia—as yesterday Jess had assured her she did—then certainly Claire would organise a car to meet her. At the back entrance to the castle? Surely. Why so early? To avoid the Press? Yes, she understood that, too.

Those arrangements had been made yesterday, with her head.

And forgotten last night, with her heart.

She checked her watch in the stillness. Raoul stirred

a little and murmured as she moved away from him. For a moment she thought he'd wake—but he settled again.

It was too late to ring Claire to stop the car. She'd have already left from Vesey.

She needed to go out and find her. Apologise. Tell her she was staying.

Was she staying?

Yes, her heart screamed. Raoul… Maybe Raoul loved her?

But how could he be thinking that, when he'd known her for such a short time? She'd thought she'd loved Warren. How could she be sure that this was different?

It was different.

But to leave Dominic's home country…

She turned in the bed, away from her husband. The fire was still glowing, sending a soft light over the room, but the first faint tinges of morning were turning the windows grey and bleak.

She slid out of bed and went to the window.

For a long time she stood there, staring outward over the grey, pre-dawn sea.

A princess in her tower?

This was a fairy tale, she thought. An impossibility. Real women didn't marry princes and become princesses.

Real women didn't get happy ever after.

This was a marriage of convenience. She knew that. The love and laughter of the night before had simply camouflaged it for a little. Now the greyness of the morning was hauling back the thick blanket of depression that had hung over her since Dominic's death.

'Who do you think you are?' she demanded of herself. 'A real-life princess? Be serious.'

Still...

She looked back at Raoul and he was waking, reaching for her and finding her gone. His eyes were open and he was smiling and her heart twisted within.

Any minute now he'd be irrevocably tied. Any minute now he'd fall in love.

She had already.

'Come back to bed,' he told her, holding out his hand in an imperious order. 'My wife.'

His wife.

How could that be? She was no one's wife. She was no one's mother. She'd told herself that after Warren's betrayal; after Dominic's loss. She'd had enough pain to last a lifetime. How could she expose herself to more?

She couldn't. That was why she'd made this offer to Raoul. He could safely use her as his wife in name only, because she intended to be no one's wife and no one's mother forever.

Could one night's love and laughter change her mind?

Raoul was watching her, his eyes concerned. 'What is it, my love?'

'It's all been so fast.'

'It has,' he said softly. 'But I'm old enough to believe in magic. Aren't you?'

'I don't know.'

'Magic has happened for me,' he murmured. 'You asked me why I hadn't married before? I thought I didn't want to marry. But Jess, if I'd met you ten years ago…'

'Don't,' she begged, and as he made to rise she backed a little. 'No.'

'No?'

'My head's having trouble holding this in.'

'And your heart?'

'That's the trouble,' she told him, seriously, knowing that he wouldn't push. 'My heart is jumping round like a stupid jumping bean. There's Dominic…'

'Jess, I'm not asking you to be unfaithful to Dominic,' he said gently. 'Dominic is your son. He's your love. Your baby. He'll always have the place of honour in your heart, and in mine also. His presence will stay in our family with love. Jess, can we be family? Can you let us share?'

She was so close to tears. They were threatening to spill and if they did she knew he'd reach for her and take her and she'd let herself sink into him.

No. She needed time.

'I'll just… Raoul, I'll just go down and check on the alpacas.'

'To give yourself space?'

He understood. Of course he understood, but somehow that made it worse.

'Please…'

'Go, my Jess,' he told her. 'Go and ask Balthazar and Matilda what you should do. But I suspect they'll tell you… Wrap yourself in love, my heart.' And then he smiled, his eyes caressing her from the top of her head to the tip of her—bare—toes. 'But maybe also wrap yourself in something a little more tangible? Like clothes?'

Why did he have to smile like this? It made her heart twist so much it hurt. It made the sane, sensible—grey?—Jessica want to leap right back into bed with him.

She grabbed a towel and she glowered, using her glower to keep him at bay. 'I have a choice between a wedding dress and a towel,' she managed, searching for lightness. 'The men from the ministry will be shocked. But it might give me some peace. I'll tell them I'm going back to my apartment to find some clothes. They can hardly argue.'

'And you'll come straight back to me after your…consultation? Your quiet time with your alpacas?'

'Y…yes.'

And then she hesitated. If a decision had to be made, then she had to know the facts. 'They can go home now, anyway, can't they?' she asked. 'The men from the ministry? I'd imagine we're well and truly compromised.'

His face stilled. 'We are at that.'

'Nothing can undo this marriage?'

'Unless you decide you want out. Jess, you can't really be thinking…'

'I don't know what I'm thinking.' Her voice was

almost a wail. 'All I know is that I can't think while I'm staring at you.'

'Really?' he said—hopefully—and her heart twisted all over again. All she wanted was to abandon her towel and dive straight back between the sheets. But...

'I need space. Raoul...'

'I understand,' he said gently. 'I won't push you any faster than you want to go. You go and talk to your babies.' He smiled again, a caress all by itself. 'At least now that you're gone I have room in this tiny bed to stretch my toes. Oh, and Jess...'

'Yes?'

'I think that I love you. I think maybe that I love you forever.'

Forever. The word hung over her head, and it was suddenly terrifying.

She stared at him for a long moment—and then she fled.

She opened the door expecting to run the gauntlet of suits, but the suits were gone. They'd have been thinking this arrangement was ridiculous, she decided, and as soon as it was apparent that she and Raoul really had spent the night together they'd have headed home.

Well, it *was* ridiculous. The place was running on outmoded laws—laws that Raoul could now change. He could do it because of her.

But not *with* her.

The trickle of fear that had crept through her while she lay in the bed was now turning to a flood. She'd been swept away, she thought desperately.

She'd fallen for a gentle smile, for a sweet prince, and she'd been seduced into something she'd promised to avoid for the rest of her life.

Loving.

Space. She had to have space.

She had thirty minutes before Claire would be here. Thirty minutes to think.

The palace was deserted. There'd been too much celebrating last night for anyone to be stirring now.

There was no one and no one and no one.

Back in her apartment she showered fast and donned jeans, windcheater and jacket. The morning was cool and no one had lit the fire in her apartment. Well, why would they?

Her suitcase was standing inside the opened wardrobe. Waiting?

She could leave now, she thought. She could meet Claire's car and she could go. The sensible Jessica Devlin would do just that.

But the sensible Jessica Devlin was having trouble.

She looked at the suitcase for a long minute, trying to let her jumbled thoughts settle.

No.

'I'll leave,' she said, softly to herself. 'Or... probably I'll leave. But not like this. I need to talk to Raoul for longer. If...*when* I leave, I need to say goodbye to him, and to Louise and Henri and Edouard. I'll find Claire and tell her I need more time.

'If you spend more time with Raoul then he'll change your mind.

'Good. That's really good,' she told her suitcase.

'Maybe I'm being a coward, not giving him that opportunity. Meanwhile you stay where you are.' And she slammed her wardrobe door on her suitcase before she could change her mind.

Alpacas.

Swiftly she made her way down the back stairs, outside into the cool morning, and across to the stables.

She reached the stable door, and walked through to the alpacas' stall.

And paused.

Balthazar and Matilda were asleep in the hay, but they weren't alone.

Edouard was there, too. They formed a confused ball of child and alpaca, three babies curled together for comfort and for warmth.

And there was more.

A mound of bedding had been piled into the corner. Soft blankets and a pile of pillows were mounded in the fresh-smelling hay. Louise was there, curled into sleep, and the strain she'd worn on her face for all the time Jess had known her was gone. She looked years younger, Jess thought. She had her grandson and she could move on.

And Henri… Louise's butler was asleep beside her, a chivalrous knight guarding his lady at rest.

The royal family of Alp'Azuri.

Jess stood and stared down at them all, and suddenly she was fighting back those stupid tears again. She bit them back with fury. She didn't cry. She never cried.

She was crying now.

Why?

How many times since Dominic died had she looked at families? At mothers pushing strollers, at fathers with toddlers on their shoulders, families laughing, playing, living. Raoul had this wonderful, loving family. Edouard was safe.

But Dominic wasn't here, and the thought broke her heart. For if Dominic wasn't here, what right did she have to stay? It was a betrayal.

She wanted her baby so much it was physical anguish, and he wasn't here, and how could she be part of any family without him?

The ache in her heart grew heavier, harder, and she backed out of the stables with tears streaming down her face.

Dominic.

The longing for him was so awful that she felt sick.

What was she doing, thinking she could possibly start again? How could she fill her heart with someone who wasn't Dominic? How could she cuddle Edouard, maybe even start a new little life…?

She couldn't. The greyness was back with a vengeance. She delved into her jacket pocket to find a handkerchief and her fingers found…

Her passport.

All her documents.

She'd taken them with her yesterday, the morning of her marriage. They were still here.

She stared down at them. Then, below her in the

valley, she saw a tiny car, growing bigger as it grew closer.

Claire.

How could she go?

How could she stay?

She couldn't. She turned back and glanced from where she'd come.

It took courage to start again, and she didn't have it.

Dominic's ashes were back in Australia.

She was going home.

'Mama?'

Louise woke as Raoul called her name. For a moment Louise was confused. There was a piece of hay tickling her face. She was warm, she was more comfortable than she'd ever felt in her life and she felt just wonderful.

Jess had given her this.

She'd checked Edouard before she'd gone to bed last night and found him fretting about his alpacas. So she and Edouard—and of course Sebastian-Bear—had set off on a torchlight expedition to the stables. They'd found Henri trying to feed them.

He'd finally succeeded, but in the end they hadn't wanted to settle. Edouard had been distressed so Henri had suggested they stay.

So they'd stayed. Well, why not? Her son was married. She could stay in this castle and raise her grandson. There was light in Louise's world as there hadn't been for a very long time.

And at some time in the night Henri's hand had caught hers and something more had changed. This elderly widower who'd been her faithful servant for so long was suddenly so much more.

It was right. Jess had given her this, she thought, lying on the straw, gazing up at her son, smiling…

'Wow,' Raoul was saying. His face was strained, she thought, but he was taking in what was before him with a sense of awe. 'This is some bedroom.'

'We camped here,' Edouard told him proudly, waking up in an instant at the sound of his uncle's voice. 'And we're going to do it again tonight. Do you want to camp, too?'

'Maybe,' Raoul told him, but the strain was obvious in his voice. He turned back to Louise. 'Mama…'

'Henri and I are getting married,' she said, serenely, and he blinked—but then he smiled.

'That's wonderful. You ought to have done it years ago.'

'Henri wouldn't,' she told him. 'But now… I told him if you could marry Jess after knowing her for only one day then I could marry Henri after knowing him for thirty years.'

Great. It was great but he needed to move on to things of even more import. 'Mama, has Jess been here?'

'No.'

'Yes, she has,' Edouard said and they all stared.

'She came in for a minute a long, long time ago,' Edouard ventured. 'I pretended I was asleep. And then I was again so it was all right.'

'You saw her?'

'Mm. She stood and looked down at me and she was crying.'

'Crying,' Raoul said, and his heart stilled. His Jess was crying.

'Can't you find her?' Louise was pushing herself upright from the straw. She could see the worry in his eyes. 'The palace is big.'

'Mama, she was crying.'

'So...'

'So maybe she's left us.'

'How could she have left us?' Louise demanded, confused. 'Raoul, what are you talking about?'

'Her return plane ticket was booked for this morning,' Henri ventured, trying—with some difficulty— to turn himself back into a dignified servant. 'She was only supposed to be in this country for ten days. I did ask her if she'd cancelled her booking and she said it was taken care of. But...' He hesitated as if he didn't want to say the words, but they had to be said. 'Maybe she intended to take the flight after all.'

Silence. Then,

'Do you love her?' Louise asked into the stillness.

'I think...'

'You think that you do.'

'I told her I thought I was falling...'

'But you haven't fallen? You haven't fallen yet?'

'Mama...'

There was another long silence. Then, 'Well, it was only a wedding of convenience, after all,' Louise said, watching her son's face. 'If it ends this morning, is there any harm done? If you're not really sure you love her.'

Not really sure. What kind of stupid statement was that?

'What time is the flight?' he snapped.

'I don't know,' Henri told him. 'But I'd imagine she's probably taken the daily connection to London which leaves at ten. Has she taken her luggage?'

'At ten?' He glanced at his watch. 'Ten!'

'But if you're not really sure,' Louise started but he was no longer listening.

He'd started to run.

It was a long journey down the mountain to Vesey Airport. Claire herself hadn't made the trip. She'd sent a driver, an inarticulate man who listened to rap music so loud that Jess could hear it through his headphones. He wasn't the least bit bothered as to whom he was carrying as a passenger.

For which Jess was inordinately grateful. She wasn't in the mood for small talk. She sat, huddled in the back seat, feeling small and cowardly.

'You didn't even say goodbye,' she told herself. 'To anybody.

'If I had, then Raoul would have talked me into staying.

'So what's wrong with that?

'I can't start again. I can't. And here, in this place…with such a man…you must see it's impossible.'

If anyone could have heard her they would have

thought she was crazy, but her driver's headphones were impervious to outside interference. She could talk at will.

But she didn't talk any more. She'd run out of arguments.

She sat and stared at nothing. She was a coward and she knew it.

But there were no arguments left.

Airports were the loneliest places in the world.

Jess booked in. No luggage. No fuss. She now had three hours to kill.

A middle-aged lady came up to her, polite and deferential. 'Excuse me, dear, but aren't you the lady who...?'

Jess stared at her blankly.

The lady stared some more and then gave an embarrassed titter.

'Oh, my dear, I'm sorry. It's just for a minute the resemblance to our new princess seemed very marked. I thought you must be related.'

She motioned to the stacks of newspapers which were selling like hot cakes from every news vendor. On the front, a truly regal couple.

Prince Raoul and his bride.

'No relation,' Jess said. She managed a weak, embarrassed smile and the lady gave her a weak, embarrassed smile back. But thoughtful. As if she wasn't quite sure.

No matter. Jess bought a coffee and a newspaper and settled to read.

FAIRY-TALE WEDDING, the headlines screamed.

JUST WHAT THE DOCTOR ORDERED.

PRINCE RAOUL, A MAN OF THE PEOPLE.

The last caught her attention. The article was based on previous knowledge of Raoul. There was a description of his medical qualifications and skills that made her feel insignificant in the face of such ability. Then there was the rest of the article, based on an interview they'd had with him yesterday.

In it Raoul outlined his hopes and his plans for this country. His intentions to transform the hospitals, the schools, the living conditions of the country's impoverished elderly.

He finished with the words, 'With Princess Jessica's help, all of these things are possible.'

'You've had my help,' she whispered to his photograph. 'Now you're on your own.'

She read on. Inside was a photograph of Edouard. 'We're so grateful to Princess Jessica,' Louise was quoted as saying. 'Edouard will now have a grandmother. He needs a mother, but it's not possible. We're all he has.'

He needs a mother. Jess stared down into the small boy's tentative smile, and she didn't smile back.

She couldn't.

Because of Dominic?

'I can't expose myself to that sort of pain,' she said out loud.

'How selfish is that?

'Really selfish. But that's just the way you are.'

An elderly couple at the next table were looking at

her strangely and she gave them an embarrassed smile. Talking to yourself. The first sign of madness. She was going nuts.

Her cell-phone rang.

Who…?

The only person to have her number was Cordelia, and why would her cousin ring?

Maybe she's found out about the wedding, Jess thought, and she didn't answer.

But the ringing went on. It stopped and started again. The lady at the table opposite leaned over and said, 'Excuse me, dear, your phone is ringing.'

She sighed—but finally she answered.

And of course she'd given the number to one person other than Cordelia. The rumbling voice was unmistakable.

'Your Highness? Am I speaking to the lady who bought my twins? The wife of our prince?'

The farmer.

'Yes.' She cleared her throat and tried to focus. 'Yes, it is.'

'Angel's in trouble. My Angel.' There was a sound very like a sob from the other end of the line. 'The mother of the twins.'

'What's wrong?' she said cautiously, and her question started a flood.

'Oh, Your Highness, I brought Angel home, but by the time she got here she was looking over her shoulder as if she'd forgotten something. And then she refused to drink…and we'd walked for so long…and she refuses to eat. And now she'll hardly stand. And this morning my wife and I are to leave. My daughter is due to have a baby right now and my wife says we go or she'll divorce me and how can I leave my Angel?'

There was no doubt about it. He was sobbing.

'Maybe you should ring the palace,' she told him. This was Raoul's problem, she thought, feeling dizzy. This was not her problem. She was going home.

'There's no one at the palace who will speak to me,' he told her. 'There's a receptionist who says no calls are being taken. And it's in an hour that we need to catch the train, and my Angel's dying and how can I leave her like this?'

The same way I did, Jess thought bitterly. You just walk away.

'I'm sure they still need their mother,' the farmer told her. 'I should have tried harder. I jumped into selling them because it seemed the easy solution. I should have had courage.'

Ouch.

'Please, Your Highness, can you help? You're at the castle. You could organise a horse trailer and take Angel back to her babies. If you manage to save her then she's yours. Your wedding gift. And if you don't…how much better to have tried and failed than not to have tried? Please, Your Highness, will you try?'

There was a long, long silence.

'Are you still there?' he asked.

'I'm thinking,' she managed. 'Hush.'

He hushed.

She thought some more.

Ouch!

Angel was dying because she'd lost her babies.

If she went back now… All it took was courage.

'Can I do it, Dominic?' she asked out loud; right out loud, so that people were turning to see who she was talking to. 'Can I start over? Can I possibly let myself love again?'

There was a moment's hush from those around her. Then,

'Sure you can, sweetheart,' someone told her from the other side of the table, and she realised that she had an audience.

'Loving again is what life is all about,' someone else said. 'The more you love, the more you get loved.'

'You sound like a fortune cookie,' someone else said, and everybody laughed.

But they were with her. The people around her were smiling in sympathy. All these people—this odd assortment of random airport humanity, some of whom would have been lucky in love, but there must be others whom tragedy had hit. Somehow they'd picked themselves up and kept going, and maybe it was those who'd been hit worst who were giving her advice now.

'I can try,' she told the assemblage, almost defiant. 'I can go back and think about it. Maybe it could work.'

'Of course it'll work.' The farmer clearly had no idea what was happening, but he was prepared to stick in his oar in any way that sounded even vaguely optimistic.

'I might need help,' she said, and the middle-aged woman who'd thought she was Princess Jessica touched her arm. Clearly she was wondering if help meant leading her gently to a lunatic asylum.

'What sort of help?'

'I need a car,' Jess told her. And then she took a deep breath. 'I need to hire a car with an alpaca trailer attached. Right now.'

CHAPTER TWELVE

SHE should be driving on this side of the road. Surely?

She was back where this had all started. The road was spiralling around snow-capped mountains, with the sea crashing a hundred feet below.

As it had before.

There were mediaeval castles, ancient fishing villages, lush pastures dotted with long-haired goats and alpacas—every sight seemingly designed to take the breath away.

She was past losing breath over this scenery.

The twist she'd just taken had given her a fleeting glimpse of the home of the Alp'Azuri royal family. Built of glistening white stone, set high on the crags overlooking the sea, the castle's high walls, its turrets and its towers looked straight out of a fairy tale.

Yeah, right. Not such a fairy tale. Raoul's home.

But she wasn't concentrating on Raoul's home. Up above she'd caught a glimpse of a brilliant-yellow sports car, coming fast.

She wasn't even going to think about what side of the road it was on this time. She was driving an ancient rent-a-heap and she was towing an even more ancient horse-trailer. She made a really big target.

Carefully she pulled off the road, onto a verge which was wider than the one she'd pulled onto when she'd crashed with Sarah. She was safe here, whatever side of the road the car was on.

The Lamborghini came around the bend fast, but not so fast to make it unsafe. It was a truly elegant sports car.

It was on the right side of the road.

It was a yellow Lamborghini.

Raoul.

The hood was down. Raoul was concentrating on the road.

Jessica's window was also down. As the Lamborghini swept past she stared across.

Raoul flicked a glance sideways and Comte Marcel came close to getting his way after all. The Prince Regent of Alp'Azuri came really, really close to driving straight off a cliff.

Somehow he didn't crash. Somehow Raoul managed to park, backing up until the Lamborghini was at rest beside the battered heap of junk Jess was driving. He stared across, unable to believe that he'd found her. She was looking across at him with wide, grave eyes that held an expression he couldn't read.

'You've come back,' he said, stupidly, and she nodded.

'I had to bring Angel.'

'Right.' He didn't understand but he wasn't arguing.

He was in his car. She was in hers. It was a thoroughly unsatisfactory arrangement which needed to be corrected immediately. It was easy enough for him to get out of his car—it was done in seconds—but that still left her.

'Jess, will you get out of the car?'

'Why?'

'I want to kiss you.'

'Um… It's just a marriage of convenience,' she said tentatively, mechanically, as if she wasn't sure what she was feeling.

'Like hell it is.' He tugged at the door. It didn't open. 'You've locked the door.'

'Only the passenger door opens. You have to climb over the gear stick to get in or out.'

'Well, climb over the gear stick.'

'Why?'

'I told you. I want to kiss you.'

'You're not mad because I ran away?'

'I'm mad because you haven't climbed over the gear stick.' He strode around the back of the trailer to reach the passenger door. Angel stuck her head out over the trailer gate and she pushed her nose in his neck. He jumped a foot.

'Why is Angel here?' He took a deep breath, regrouped and abandoned Angel. 'No, never mind. Where were we?' He hauled open the passenger door.

Jess was coming out feet first.

He wanted the other end.

'Why do you want to kiss me?' she asked, muffled by the car seat.

'You're my wife. I love you.'

'You love me?'

'Of course I love you,' he told her. 'Of course I do.' She was out, and he was turning her to face him.

'Last night…you never said you did,' she whispered cautiously. 'You said you might.'

'That's because you wouldn't let me win at slot-cars.' He was tugging her into his arms, holding her close. 'I never tell anyone I love them when they won't let me win at slot-cars.'

'And if I let you win?'

'Then I'll love you forever and ever.' He bent to kiss her—but she pushed away. Just a little.

'Raoul…'

Laughter faded. The joy at finding her took a back step as he recognised the seriousness and the deep doubts in her voice. He heard the echo of tears and he drew back. His hands were cupping her face, his eyes were searching hers and he thought: how could he have ever thought that he might in time come to love this woman? He loved her with his whole heart. Right now.

'Jess, you can win at slot-cars any time you want,' he said, and he couldn't keep his voice steady. It was doing this quaver thing that he didn't recognise—that he couldn't control. 'I've been a fool,' he said and in that instant any hint of levity fell away. There was only room for truth between them, and both of them knew it. 'Jess, darling Jess, I love you now, with all my heart, with everything I have. You are my wife, Jess, whether or not you want to stay with me. But I so hope you do. I do so hope you can. When I thought you'd left me… Oh, Jess.'

'I don't…'

'It's Dominic, isn't it?' he asked, and his hands caressed her face, willing the pain to disappear from her eyes. 'Jess, loving again isn't a betrayal of Dominic. How can it be?'

'I don't know,' she whispered and he heard the agony of indecision. 'It just seems…wrong.'

'I know. It's far too soon.' He was seeking desperately to understand her pain. He was smoothing her face, tracing her spent tears. Loving her with his whole heart. 'For you to lose your baby and then have us thrust on you; it's far too fast. But it's happened. Magically it's happened, my love.' He hesitated. 'Surely Dominic wouldn't want your world to stay grey.'

'No. He wouldn't.'

He hadn't got it right. She was suddenly angry, pushing him away in distress. 'Of course he wouldn't. Dominic didn't want anything except to be. To live. But he didn't. I couldn't save him. And he can't be part of this. How can I have a happy ending when he can't?'

There was a moment's hush. The waves washed in and out beneath them while he tried desperately, frantically, to find the right words.

'And Lisle can't,' he said softly, at last. 'And Jean-Paul and Cherie and Sarah. And the people I'm working with in Somalia. So much death. It eats away at you. I know it, my Jess, and I hate it. The waste.'

'I don't... I just want my Dominic.'

It was a wail of aching sorrow and it was too much. He pulled her against his shoulder and he stroked the close-cropped curls and kissed the top of her head. She shuddered against him and he held her closer.

'Did you cry, my love?' he asked softly. 'When Dominic died—did you cry then?'

'I... No. I couldn't.'

'Yet this morning you cried.'

'When I looked at Edouard. With his family.'

Damn, his heart was breaking just listening to her. If he could take this pain away... He'd cut his own heart out to spare her this desolation.

But he couldn't. The death of her son was something that would stay with her forever and all he could do was be there for her.

'You know, families are strange things,' he said, softly into her curls. He was barely touching her with his hands, aware that at any minute she could pull away. She was leaning into him but his hands didn't lock her to him.

The sea air was warm on their skin. The sound of the surf was a gentle hush-hush of a backdrop. But he wasn't noticing. He was fighting, and he was fighting with everything he had.

'In Somalia...' he told her, going sideways to her desolation but sensing it was maybe the right thing to do. 'In Somalia the people are being decimated by AIDS. I see tragedies every day as I work there. So many orphans. So many deaths. But you know, the inter-aid agencies have gone down the road of adopt-

ing children out of their own countries and they've
drawn back. Because no matter how dreadful the circumstances, no matter how many deaths there are in
families, families seem to reform. Regroup. Two families become one. Two teenage girls, friends, get together to raise siblings. Grandmas and uncles and second cousins once removed are stepping in to pick up
the pieces. I've watched it over and over, with awe.
And you know what, my Jess? The only linking they
have is love.'

'But…'

'Don't stop me,' he told her, still stroking her hair.
Aching for her to understand this with him. 'Because
I'm only just figuring this out for myself. Since Lisle's
death, I've been an outsider looking in. I didn't think
I had any love left to give. But of course I did. Love
expands to fill the void. Edouard needs my love. My
mother and Henri… I love them and they love me.
And I love my memories of Lisle. How could I have
said I had no more love when I still love my twin?
She's part of my life forever. Dominic's death has
brought you over to my country, despairing, and his
life will stay in my heart for always as well. Because
of you, my darling Jess, Dominic will live on, with
us, with those we love now and with those who come
after. But only if we let that legacy live on, my love.
Love can't look back all the time. What I've found
with you…it's given me so much joy that I feel I can
face anything. With you. Because most of all, best of
all, greatest of all, I love you.'

He set her back from him then, just a little, holding

her at arm's length so he could see her face. She stared up at him with eyes that were unfathomable and he didn't know, he couldn't tell…

'I'm asking you to give me a chance,' he whispered. 'I'm asking you to let me teach you that we can be a family. That we're not excluding anyone or dishonouring anyone. If you agree, if you let me love you, then we'll be taking our love for Dominic and for Lisle and Edouard and Mama and Henri—and cousin Cordelia and whoever else comes along—but most of all we'll be taking our love for each other and we'll be moving forward. I love you so much, my beautiful Jessica, and I want more than anything else in the world to make you happy. Will you give me that chance? Can we move forward…together?'

There was no answer. She was reaching up for him. She had her hands in his hair, tugging his face down to hers.

'Is this for real?' she asked. 'Is this truly how you feel about me?'

'How can you doubt it?'

'It's just…it's a bit of a shock,' she told him.

'Why?'

'You see, I've been driving up this road for the last hour, pushing this stupid alpaca into the trailer, bringing her home, and every step of the way I've been thinking exactly what you're thinking.'

'You're kidding.'

'I never kid,' she told him. 'Not when you're concerned. I've been missing Dominic so much, but then when I had to leave I thought I was adding yet another loss to my collection. I wanted you so much it just…cut. And now, here you are, saying all the right things, making it…fine.'

'Fine?'

'It's not a great description for how I'm feeling,' she whispered. 'But it's the best I can do without a scriptwriter. Does being a princess make me eligible to have a scriptwriter?'

'You're doing just fine on your own,' he told her. 'But if you want a scriptwriter you shall have one. You shall have anything you wish. Forever.' He smiled. And smiled and smiled and smiled.

So…' Her nose was two inches from his nose and she was smiling almost as much as he was. 'Let's get this straight. Even if I don't let you win at slot-cars, you'll still love me.'

The sun was coming out, he thought, a blazing sun that warmed every inch of his being. She was so close. She was laughing into his eyes, her eyes were wet with tears and she was his. His own, his lovely Jessica!

'I'll love you forever and ever anyway,' he told her. 'Though I may have to sabotage your slot-car. Now, have you any other questions?'

'No.'

'Then how about hushing to be kissed?'

'What a truly excellent idea,' she murmured and that was the last thing either of them could say for a very long time.

* * *

'Well!' It was a woman's voice. American. 'The things you see.'

'It's local colour,' her friend said, dubiously.

There was a tour bus right by them—the kind that took tourists on a See-Europe-in-Ten-Days type of tour. The combination of Jessica's car and Raoul's Lamborghini meant the bus had been brought to a halt and the bus driver was honking for them to move.

Which might well happen when they finished kissing. Eventually. Maybe.

The bus doors were opening now, and, as Jess and Raoul drew reluctantly apart, tourists started piling out. There was a great view of the castle from here, and the bus passengers had obviously demanded to use the opportunity for photographs.

'They say the prince got married yesterday,' someone said. 'If I used my telephoto lens I might see royalty.'

'Not from here,' someone else said.

'Hey, you,' the bus driver told Raoul. 'Move that heap of junk.' Then he eyed the Lamborghini. 'And that, too.'

'Not until I've finished proposing,' Raoul said, and went back to kissing Jessica.

'Proposing,' Jess said breathlessly, in between kisses. 'What are you proposing?'

'This morning,' he said, softly, in her hair, 'after you left my bed, I remembered that I'd forgotten. You proposed to me.' His arms held her, tightly, as if she was the most precious thing in the world. 'But I forgot to propose to you. Jess, this started out as a marriage of convenience but that lasted a whole two minutes before I realised that I'd married the most wonderful woman in the world. That I love you more than life itself. Those we've lost, Jess—they're still with us. They're part of us and they'll stay with us as we stay together. As we live together. As man and wife.'

'That's...that's proposing?' she whispered.

'No, it's not,' he told her and promptly fell to one knee.

'Hey, look at this,' said their first American tourist and nudged her friend.

'It's Jessica.' The yell went up from back up the road. Edouard, his hand held by Henri on one side and Louise on the other, had found their way blocked by the coach and had come the last few steps on foot. 'It's Jessica. And Uncle Raoul's on the ground.'

'He's proposing,' the American said and everyone in the tour group focused.

'He's proposing,' Louise whispered. 'Oh, Jess.'

'Wait for us.' It was a roar, and they turned to see a mêlée of newsmen. Clearly, Louise and Henri and Edouard had been followed. There were professional photographers here now. One edged his way in front of the American tourist and got a swipe from her handbag for his pains.

'This is my spot.'

'But if His Highness is proposing...'

'His Highness?'

'This is the Prince Regent of Alp'Azuri,' the photographer said. 'And his family.'

'Well, why didn't you say so?' the woman exclaimed. 'Go ahead,' she said to Raoul. 'Don't mind us.'

'I won't,' Raoul said. 'Jess…'

'Can you move a little to the right?' the photographer called.

The photographer was ignored. 'Jessie…'

'Yes?' She was torn between tears and laughter. She was stranded in the most beautiful place in the world. She was surrounded by the people she loved—and a whole lot of people she'd never seen in her life. And Raoul was saying,

'Will you be my wife?'

It was maybe the weirdest proposal that had ever been made in the history of the Alp'Azuri royal family.

It was the most excellent proposal Jess had ever heard.

And there was only one answer.

She looked down at the man she loved. He gazed up at her and his eyes said it all. She needed courage to take this leap, but he was right here to catch her, forever and ever and ever.

'Yes, my love,' she told him. 'Yes, I'll be your wife. Forever.'

It was the weirdest day.

It was the best day. A day for moving on…

They'd been surrounded by celebrations, by fuss, by laughter and happiness all this day. Now finally the population of the castle had gone to bed. Soon Jess and Raoul would return to the bridal suite for the real beginning of their married life. But for now...

Now they walked out under the stars and entered the stables.

Angel was kneeling in the hay, and nuzzling her udder were two tiny crias. Matilda and Balthazar.

It had taken time to reunite these three. For a start they'd had to get rid of their audience. Then they'd led a shaky Angel into the stables. For a moment she'd nuzzled the babies, uncertain.

Balthazar had pushed his tiny head under her udder and drunk.

Angel had licked him and then lowered her head into the manger and eaten.

But then Matilda had tried.

Angel had turned and pushed the baby away.

One baby, it had seemed, was enough.

But Raoul was made of sterner stuff. He lifted Balthazar away from the teat. He held him at arm's length and Angel bleated her distress.

Jess shepherded Matilda back to the teat.

Angel pushed her away.

Over and over.

Half an hour. The tiny Balthazar was frantic and Matilda was starting to wilt.

And then...Angel finally lifted her head and stared from Jess to Raoul and back again.

'Come on,' Raoul told her. 'You have enough heart for two babies.'

Angel seemed to sigh. She turned back to Matilda,

who was still by her side. She nosed her, licked her—
and finally she let her attach to her teat.

Gently, Raoul had placed Balthazar down. He wriggled his way under, and two babies had been united
with their mother.

Now they walked over to the stables, half expecting
their happy ending to be not so happy—for her to have
rejected one again.

But the three alpacas were fast asleep on the hay.
A twin lay on either side of the udder. Angel stirred
and looked up as they came in and gave a sleepy alpaca yawn.

'We've done it,' Raoul said in satisfaction. 'We've
united a family.

'So we have,' Jess said, softly, from the blessing of
her husband's arms.

'So we have.'

And two months later...another ceremony.

Two vials of ashes. One taken from a vault in Paris.
There had never seemed an appropriate time, an appropriate place. The other taken from the children's
wall of a cemetery in Sydney.

Lisle and Dominic.

They were gathered together, this day. The calm old
priest who'd blessed this marriage, Raoul and Jess,
and all who loved them.

This was perfect, Jess thought.

They were in the walled kitchen garden. All around
the edges were roses, wisteria, jasmine, hollyhocks,
delphiniums, a riot of brilliant colour. In the centre

were rows and rows of vegetables, enough to feed a small village. Hens—chooks?—were clucking around the edges. Doves were fluttering around the dovecote in the far corner. Through the gaps in the ancient stone walling you could see and hear the sea.

This kitchen garden was no formal garden. It was used every day, by everyone who lived in this castle. Edouard played here with his baby alpacas—though they had to be kept sternly from the lettuces. The servants gossiped here. Louise and Henri sat and held hands and watched Edouard play. Raoul and Jess sat here in the moonlight. And soon... In not so many months, maybe there'd be a crib out here, where a little one could have a daily dose of sun.

Home. Home is where the heart is, Jess thought dreamily. Home is here.

There were even two cracked and blackened pots arranged artistically on a garden bench, which Raoul refused to remove because 'Every time I look at them I remember how wonderful life is'.

And now...

The priest said the last few words of blessing. Louise unfastened the lid of one urn and gave it to Raoul.

Jess unfastened her own small urn.

They turned together, hand in hand and faced the sea. They lifted their urns and they let the ash drift across the garden on the soft sea breeze to land where it would.

The urns were empty. Jess turned and she held her

husband tight, and once again she shed tears. But this time there was no desolation.

This was right.

Lisle and Dominic had come home.

With their families.

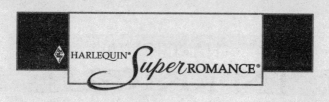
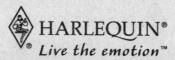

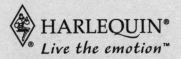

Harlequin Historicals®
Historical Romantic Adventure!

From rugged lawmen and valiant knights to defiant heiresses and spirited frontierswomen, Harlequin Historicals will capture your imagination with their dramatic scope, passion and adventure.

Harlequin Historicals . . . they're too good to miss!

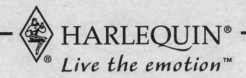
HARLEQUIN®
Live the emotion™

HARLEQUIN®
AMERICAN *Romance*®

Upbeat, All-American Romances

HARLEQUIN®
flipside

Romantic Comedy

Harlequin Historicals®
Historical Romantic Adventure!

HARLEQUIN®
INTRIGUE

Romantic Suspense

HARLEQUIN®

HARLEQUIN ROMANCE®

The essence of modern romance

HARLEQUIN®
Presents

Seduction and Passion Guaranteed!

HARLEQUIN® *Super* ROMANCE®

Emotional, Exciting, Unexpected

Temptation

Sassy, Sexy, Seductive!